Radium Halos

(Senseless Series Part II)
By W.J. May
Copyright 2014 W.J. May

All rights reserved. No part of this publication may be reproduced, stored in or introduced into a retrieval system, or transmitted, in any form, or by any means (electronic, mechanical, photocopying, recording, or otherwise) without the prior written permission of both the copyright owner and the above publisher of this book.

This is a work of fiction. Names, characters, places, brands, media, and incidents are either the product of the author's imagination or are used fictitiously. The author acknowledges the trademarked status and trademark owners of various products referenced in this work of fiction, which have been used without permission. The publication/use of these trademarks is not authorized, associated with, or sponsored by the trademark owners.

Also by W.J. May

Hidden Secrets Saga
Seventh Mark - Part 1
Seventh Mark - Part 2

The Chronicles of Kerrigan
Rae of Hope
Dark Nebula

The Senseless Series
Radium Halos
Radium Halos - Part 2

Standalone
Five Shades of Fantasy
Glow - A Young Adult Fantasy Sampler
Shadow of Doubt - Part 1
Shadow of Doubt - Part 2
Four and a Half Shades of Fantasy

The Senseless Series:

Download Radium Halos part 1 For FREE

Radium Halos part 2

Website: http://www.wanitamay.yolasite.com
Facebook:
https://www.facebook.com/pages/Author-WJ-May-FAN-PAGE
Cover design by: Book Cover by Design
Book II

Chapter 1

Zoe

"The water tower?" Brent scratched at the shadow of stubble on his chin. "How we going to race—?"

"Without killing yourselves?" Heidi shook her head and crossed her arms over her chest. "Uh-uh. Dumb idea."

"Wait a minute. It's a great idea." Seth began pacing with excitement. "The tower's easily triple the height of this thing in here. The city's repainting it right now so it's got all that scaffolding up."

Kieran pointed north in the direction of the old water tower. It stood more as tourist billboard off the highway than as an actual storage tank. It still carried rain water but who knew if farmers or anyone actually used it. "I drove by yesterday and noticed some slanted trough bits set up." He shrugged. "Maybe they plan to drain it or something. Thought it would be perfect to race down."

Heidi sighed. "I don't–"

"I'm game." I cut Heidi off before her reasoning would convince me to change my mind. I wanted—no, needed—something more challenging. *To beat Brent or impress Kieran?*

Seth grabbed his sweatshirt and shoved it on over his head. "Let's go. We can discuss it on the way."

Dusk turned dark by the time we got there and walked around the tower. At least the air was warm. The engines from the cars zooming by on the nearby highway buzzed by my ears like mosquitoes. Even with the sound barrier bricks, the noise penetrated through.

Seth tossed a pebble into the nearby trees. "It might be hard to see but it means we won't get caught. The lights from the highway are giving it a decent glow but the scaffolding's on the other side."

"It's too dark and too stupid to even consider this." Heidi trailed a few feet behind us.

Rylee stopped walking and put her hands on her hips. "You stay on the ground then. Grow some cojones and stop bein' such a freakin' wimp."

My mouth fell open. "Rylee!" We were all nervous, but Rylee didn't need to be a bitch.

Kieran moved to Heidi and slipped his arm around her shoulders. "Don't worry, lass. You stay by me. They'll be fine. Watch and see." He pointed at all of us. "You all have the skills. Just believe. It's easy for me to see watching you, but they're there. I know it."

Silent, we walked to the other side of the tower. The tall grass had become dry and crackled under our feet. Paranoid, I kept staring at the ground, positive some slinking animal would come scurrying out. I knew I'd hear it beforehand, but it still gave me the heebie-jeebies. I think we were all paranoid someone would drive by or a cop would show up. No way was getting caught part of the plan.

The scaffolding went about halfway up the ball, and like Kieran had said earlier, there were two long, tube-like structures emptying into large disposal bins.

Brent jogged over to one of the bins and spread his fingers on the side metal. "Garbage, paint chips, cans, and other junk. They probably use the tubes instead of taking stuff down the ladders."

Seth stood under one of the troughs, jumped up, and hung on. Using his large frame, he shook his weight to see if it would hold. "It's strong enough." He let go and dropped back down to the ground.

I chewed my lower lip and tried to calculate how high up the scaffolding stood. Six stories? Maybe seven? Eight? It looked pretty high. "Is it just Brent and me racing?"

Rylee climbed a few rungs of the scaffolding and hugged it tight when it lurched slightly from the wind. "How about you guys go first?" She quickly crawled back down. "Then maybe Seth and me."

I inhaled a deep breath. Cars racing down the highway roared in my ears, the wind swirling through the trees and slapping against the tower distracted me, but I wanted to do this. Adrenaline rushed through my veins and wouldn't leave till I pushed it. I reached for the cold metal and started climbing.

A minute later I glanced down to see my friends. I couldn't tell if their eyes or opened mouths were bigger. "Brent! You coming... or you chicken?" I grinned. I had one up on him, on all of them, if no one else did it. I heard Heidi whisper to Rylee.

"You do know I can totally hear you. And I am not going psycho," I interrupted her. "For the record, I'm completely clear in the head." I reached inside my back pocket and tossed them my phone. "Don't drop it." I started climbing again, intentionally not looking down.

I heard Brent mumble, "Ah shit" under his breath and the ladder shifted and shook slightly from his weight. His increased heart rate and breathing echoed inside my ears. It didn't take him long to catch up to me.

Five minutes later we reached the flat boards of the scaffolding. I crawled through the small gap and sat down to catch my breath... and my courage. Brent slid beside me a moment later. I hugged my knees. He hung his legs over the edge and leaned into the lower railing. There were two railings and the boards under us were sturdy. It felt safe up here on the scaffold. The minute we stepped off would be another story.

He grinned. "You're fearless now, aren't you?"

I swallowed and rested my elbows on the railing. "Not at the moment."

"We don't have to do this."

"Trying to make me look like the wimp?" I teased. "No way. I will race you in the dark, or at a park, down the pole, or in a hole. I will not lose this race, I will not lose, Brent-I-am."

He shook his head and chuckled. "Sad. Very, very sad."

I giggled but turned quiet as I stared at the night lights of Elliot Lake and listened to the massive sounds of the night. Cars driving, people partying, watching TV, someone crying, a distinctive "I love you" shouted and then followed by laughter. I sighed. It felt like I was eavesdropping on everyone.

He followed my gaze. "There's something about being this high up... it's... it's..."

"I know what you mean." Words couldn't describe the incredible feeling.

The town shone with lights of the night in different colours and hues. Northern Lights seemed to be dancing along the edge of the sky. "I bet Rylee could see everything from up here."

"It amazing from what I can see." Brent cleared his throat as he looked away from me and across the county. "If her eyes are that much better, yeah, wow. As much as I want to leave here when I graduate, tonight makes me think this place ain't so bad."

I scanned the view and concentrated on the forest area not far from the water tower. "I plan on coming back when I'm done with university. It's a great place. I could grow old here."

"Like get married and have a fam—"

"Brent!" I grabbed his forearm and clenched it tight and pointed at the trees with my free hand. "Look! There toward the left."

A weird dancing light flickered a moment, then disappeared. It happened again twenty seconds later.

"What is that?" Brent began tapping his fingers against the metal railing, the noise echoed inside my ear canal. "There it is again. It's bigger. Wait. Now it's not disappearing."

A strange cracking mixed with a hissing kind of noise strained against my eardrums. I closed my eyes to focus and try to locate what the noise meant. My eyes popped open at the same moment Brent whispered, "Fire."

I reached for my phone. "Crap! My phone's down at ground level."

"Mine too."

"They can't see it down there because of those huge garbage bins." I tried inhaling a few deep breaths. It suddenly felt like my brain wanted to go dizzy.

Brent reacted the second before I came back to life. He pointed to the metal tube jutting out of the corner off to my right. "You go down that one. I'll use the one by the ladder." He rested his hand on my shoulder. "We'll slide down on our stomachs, okay? Just hold tight like you're going down a stair banister." His fingers trailed down my arm. "Whatever you do, don't let go."

"I won't." I tried pushing the sudden erratic butterflies back down. "You don't go and break anything." My legs and arms moved with their own will toward my corner. "Brent?"

"Yeah?" He was crawling on his hands and knees but paused to look back at me.

"Let's not tell our dads we did this."

"Gotchya." He chuckled. "Your dad'll kill me before mine's even finished yelling." He began moving again.

I listened to Kieran, Seth, Heidi, and Rylee talking below. They were arguing who should video it on their phones. They had no idea about the flames. I glanced again at the batch of trees. The flames were definitely getting bigger.

The wood boards shifted and shook slightly as all of Brent disappeared except for his hands.

I slipped my right leg through the lower railing and then my left. My hands clung tight to the railing above and I shuffled the last few inches to the trough. I squinted at its shape and crouched down. The trough was very smooth, probably about the width of my shoe.

"Screw going on my stomach," I mumbled. I clung to the rail on the scaffold with one hand and set both feet onto the hollow metal tube. I leaned like a sprinter in the starting blocks. The pole shook from the wind and gave me the feeling of a wider base. The noise created little ricochets that my ears translated into something for my eyes. Eerie silvery light. Freaky, but it let the butterflies stop trying to rip through my gut to break free.

"Brent," I whispered. "Can you see?"

"A bit. Use your hearing, Zoe." Brent swallowed. "Focus on yourself. Be careful." From the corner of my eye I saw him start to slide.

I pushed against the scaffold as hard as I could. Feet set as if I was on a skateboard, I leaned forward as far as I could. It was impossible to see Brent now from my peripheral vision but he definitely wasn't in front of me anymore.

He couldn't be far behind. Our troughs were about twenty metres apart so I knew he was close, and he hadn't fallen. Keeping my abs tight, I remembered some coach or gym teacher saying our core centre of balance lay an inch or two below our belly button. Keeping it tight seemed important to maintaining balance.

The wind whipped my hair behind me and roared against my ears, along with screams from below. My eyes watered but blinking a bunch of times helped. I focussed on staring at the trough ten meters ahead. I shifted slightly when I realized the silvery misty thing I saw against the beam had a rectangular shape in front of me.

I lost my balance when I realized it was the huge Waste Management garbage bin. My arms automatically spread wide and I regained equilibrium. That's when I saw Brent about two feet behind me and the gang jumping up and down with Seth and Rylee pointed at us and cheering.

"Jump!" Kieran shouted. To me, or Brent, or maybe both of us.

I did, about half a second before I'd have landed into the bin. In the air I tucked into a ball, ready to roll when I hit the grass.

My feet hit first and all ability to gracefully roll turned into me jarring and flopping around until I finally stopped with a mouthful of grass and dirt.

"Zoe won!" Rylee cheered.

I moaned and covered my face. "Freakin' eh!" No blood rushed from my nose and nothing appeared broken. However, my body had landed like a train wreck.

Brent. I popped my head up. He lay on his back just behind me. He leaned up on his elbows "Holy sh—"

"Th-The f-fire!" I huffed as I tried to catch the knocked out wind. I struggled to sit up.

Seth must not have heard me. He rushed over and knelt over Brent waving his phone. "I got it all on video. I can't believe Zoe stood up and you went down it like a pansy."

I grimaced as I touched my elbow. A bad strawberry burn with blood oozing down my arm brought me back to reality. "We raced down 'cause we saw a fire." Using my fingers, I signalled Rylee to toss me my phone. "We gotta call nine-one-one again."

"You're jokin'!" Heidi opened her mouth and breathed in. She coughed like she'd just tasted a mouthful of smoke. Doubling over, she waved in the direction behind the bins. "Call the fire department. I mean, your dad!"

Seth sniffed and started running. He disappeared behind the large metal box. I heard him tapping the numbers on his phone. "Dad! There's a fire not far from the water tower. No, it wasn't us. We were just hanging out and saw it."

Ignoring the pain radiating from my elbow, I pushed myself up and started chasing Seth.

"What's he saying?" Heidi ran beside me.

"His dad wants to know if we saw how it started." I continued listening to Seth, who was still at least four hundred meters away.

"Now he wants to know why we were climbing the tower. He's giving Seth crap about the dangers and stuff."

"How bad's the fire?" Kieran shouted. He had already passed us and ran by Seth.

"I barely see it through the trees." Rylee sprinted to catch up to the boys. "But there's smoke in the air. A lot. It's moving pretty fast."

"I hear it. It's louder now than from the scaffold." Sirens started far off into the distance. Too far for my liking. I glanced behind and almost stumbled. "Where's Brent?"

A sudden gust of wind blew in our direction, full of smoke and the smell of burning. The heat of the fire heading our way suddenly made everything too real. The fire was getting incredibly close.

"What?" Seth shouted as he stopped running. He bent over with his hands on his knees. Everything inside of him was pumping and pushing and begging for more oxygen.

"Brent's not with us." Panic pressed against my chest. Had he hurt himself before and not owned up to it? I went over what happened when we'd landed only moments ago.

"He's..." Kieran glanced at Rylee, who was frantically looking around. His head turned in the same direction as hers when she brought her hand to her mouth and her breath caught.

"What the heck?" She pointed to the water tower. "He's up there."

"Huh?" Seth straightened, plugged his nose, and tried not to cough. "What's he doing?"

I swung around and squinted. It was hard to see but the scraping of metal and sudden banging of hollow metal couldn't be missed. One of the troughs shifted and wobbled back and forth. Just as I realized what Brent was doing, Kieran started tearing back to the water tower.

"He's gonna get the water to flood the ground and forest. We 'ave to help him!"

Those of us still standing burst into a sprint. We raced back to tower, the distance now seeming longer this time. Sirens grew louder and a fire truck flew by on the highway, its lights flashing. Another one followed it down the exit moments later.

Brent had managed to break the top of a tube I had slid down loose from the scaffold and was rolling it.

Seth coughed and spat. "What's he doing, Rylee?"

Rylee pressed a hand against her eyebrows and looked up at. "He's got the top of the tube by a latch on the water tower. I think he's trying to hammer the handle."

To get the latch open so water would pour down. "Brent's got an idea."

"Let's get the base moved." Kieran jumped onto the bin and began kicking the base of the tube.

It took the five of us on the ground to break the trough free of the bin. It groaned in protest as it shifted a few meters. We worked without thinking or talking, all of going as fast as we could.

The noise from the fire terrified me, like it wanted to hunt us down. Heat burned against my skin and made all of us sweat. Everything was moving too fast. Ironically, the ash drifted by in a slow dance.

"Pussshhh!" Seth hollered as his muscles strained in exertion. Finally the trough broke free from a tripod stand that kept it stable near the base. The bars clamoured to the ground and the trough swung away from us toward the fire.

From above, Brent hollered, "Watch out!"

I heard the water bubble inside the tower and splash against the insides of the trough as it raced down. Brent must have managed to get the hatch open and set the trough to let the water pour down. I jumped up to try and push the base of the tube toward the forest. I could barely reach it now; only my fingers managed to make contact. It didn't budge. "Seth! Push it again. The water's coming!"

Seth ran and leapt in the air, both arms coming up and nailing the trough with perfect athletic timing. It swung wild and water ricocheted out of the spout, flying over the first trees and dumping into the forest. The trough swung a few meters to the right, and, because of the pressure from the water, moving back to the left like a clock pendulum.

Angry hissing and the sound of fire drowning sounded like music to my ears. "It's hitting the fire."

The same time I spoke, Rylee said, "I can see it."

"Fire department's on the other side fighting it as well." Brent stood beside Kieran, his arms crossed and a big goofy grin on his face.

I ran over and hugged him. "You crazy idiot!"

"Idiot?" Kieran laughed. "I'd say more along the lines of a genius. That was brilliant." He high-fived Brent.

"I saw the lower flood latch when Zoe and I were up there before. I figured it was worth a shot. How you guys moved the base was awesome." Brent opened and closed his hands into fists, then tucked them into his jean pockets.

"See!" Seth pounded Brent on the back. "I told you we make an awesome team."

Kieran glanced toward the road. "Oye! May I suggest we get our arses outta here? Don't think we want ta get caught."

"Oh, crap!" Heidi turned and started running down the path.

Everyone followed her, only to stop and turn in the opposite direction when sirens warned us someone was coming.

We sprinted about fifty metres when gravel crunching gave me the heads-up before the others. About to warn them, I never got the chance. Heidi pulled up short when a red SUV blocked the road. Rylee covered her eyes from the bright headlights.

A fireman jumped out of the driver's side and held his hand up. He held a phone in the other. "Nobody move. I'm calling the cops."

Chapter 2

"We didn't do it." Brent walked over to Heidi.

Another fire department vehicle drove up. It lurched to a stop and Seth's dad jumped out. "You kids all right?" Another firefighter jumped out of the passenger side and began climbing up the scaffold ladder.

"We're fine, Dad." Seth pointed to the fireman with the phone still by his ear. "He thinks we started the fire."

Rylee glanced at the dying fire and water still gushing from the tower. "We didn't."

"Russ, put the phone away. That's my kid. They're the ones who soaked the flames on this end."

Russ hit a button on his phone.

Seth didn't let Russ reply. "You saw what we did? Totally awesome, 'eh?"

His dad smiled. "Quick thinking, but dangerous." He shook his head. "What were you doing out here anyway?"

Russ snorted. "Not hard to guess."

Seth's dad shot him a warning look. "Some inexperienced camper called nine-one-one and said he'd dropped a gasoline canister when trying to get a bonfire going."

Russ shook his head. "Tell your kid and his friends to get a job or find something useful to do in the evenings. Not hang out where trouble seems to be finding them." He got in his truck, slammed the door shut, and spurned gravel as he drove off.

Seth's dad sighed and shook his head.

"Why couldn't you stop the fire where it started?" Seth asked his dad, refusing to acknowledge Russ's last remark.

"We got to the flames, but when the wind changed direction, suddenly we thought we were screwed. You kids... well, you basically saved the day."

"Saved the night," Heidi murmured.

"Superheroes." Seth nudged her.

His dad either hadn't heard or purposely ignored them. "Good job, but incredibly stupid and dangerous." He tapped Seth on his chest. "You better not have been drinking out here." He looked around at all of us. "You're good kids, but what in the world? The cops are going to want to know who did the damage to city property. First the mine, then PHP, and now here. You guys are going to start getting the wrong reputation." He glanced up the gravel road. "I think you need to get going."

Sirens screamed further off in the distance, a different sound to the ones from the fire trucks. I glanced at the others, unsure if we should run.

Brent, on my right, stood staring at my elbow. "You need a bandage on that."

"It's fine." I tried to pull my sleeve down to hide it.

Seth's dad stopped jabbering when the firemen climbed down from the water tower and stood by the truck. The two-way inside the cab crackled to life. Police were heading to this area.

Seth's dad raced to the truck and got in. He started the engine and did the fastest U-turn I'd ever seen. As he drove by us, he rolled the window down. "Get out of here. I'll talk to the cops and make sure Russ is on the same page." He sped away after the SUV.

We did as he said and raced out there. None of us spoke the ride home, and back at Brent's place we gathered our things and said goodnight. I think everyone needed to go over the evening on their own. I know I did. So many thoughts were racing around in my head, competing with the noises in my ears, and I had no idea how to calm them down.

The next afternoon I leaned against the biology room window when a bike engine roared to life. Rylee was skipping last class to leave with Kieran on his motorcycle. I heaved a disappointed sighed and couldn't stop myself watching as they zoomed off school property.

Trying to refocus my attention on memorizing the periodic table seemed next to impossible. My thoughts kept drifting back to Rylee. Her coy laughter as she climbed on the bike behind Kieran, the rustling of her hair as she tossed it over her shoulder before putting a helmet on and whispering she hoped he didn't mind her holding him super tight so she wouldn't fall.

Honestly, how could a hundred and eighteen chemical elements and their freakin' atomic structure be more important than a hot guy? I groaned. What about chemistry between people? More like the lack of it. I obviously didn't stand a chance if Kieran was even remotely interested in Rylee. Of course she'd be interested in the new guy. Who could blame her?

Kieran would have to be blind not to notice her. Straightening my arms to try and focus on the chart again, I swore under my breath when my bruised elbow rubbed against the desktop.

No way could I focus. Frustrated, I began picking up on everyone's conversations – those studying and others gossiping. *This freakin' sucks!* The guy I like is with the prettiest girl in town, I can't sleep because everything is too bloody loud, and when I get annoyed it's impossible to block anything out! I couldn't do it when I was calm and it magnified a hundred times when I wasn't. Rubbing my eyes against the palms of my hands, Heidi's tentative step echoed in my ears several seconds before she spoke. It gave me a moment to try and compose myself.

"Everything okay?" Heidi never missed anything. She even made the effort to whisper below normal levels.

None of us had mentioned last night at the water tower. Somehow all of us had made the consensus to wait till we were on our own after school. I slid the chart back and forth across the counter then stopped as the laminate screeched against the fake wood desk. I tried to make my face blank, praying it would be unreadable. "Yeah, I'm all right. It's just hard to concentrate with..." I pointed at my ears. Stretching my legs, I grimaced. "I think every muscle in my entire body has been ripped and shredded."

"After what you and Brent did last night, plus training, I'm not surprised. How's your elbow?"

"Bruised and ugly." I glanced down. An icky, patchy scab surrounded by purple, green, and blue throbbed on my skin and deeper to the muscle. It actually seemed to have scabbed over pretty quickly. "It'll heal. How are you feeling?"

Heidi swallowed and frowned. "I swear I can taste the lactic acid in my system from what we did yesterday. Are we going to Brent's again today?"

"I think so." Hopefully playing dumb worked. I did not want to appear obvious that I had just heard the motorcycle zoom away.

"I'll go, but no training crap. My arms are killing me. I can barely hold my pen." She pretended to lift her pencil like a weight bar and faked falling over. We started giggling, and then had to grab our sides at the same time from the sore muscles, which only made us laugh more. Class dragged, but at least we had each other to keep company.

After class, Heidi and I met up with Seth and Brent in the parking lot by my car.

"Where's Rylee?" Seth glanced around and checked his watch.

I shifted, reminded again of the motorcycle ride.

Brent saved me from answering. "She and Kieran are changing the gym around." He opened the passenger door to the Bug, "I went by my place at lunch and turned the alarm system off. Rylee bugged me all morning. When she gets an idea in her head..." He shook his head. "She was driving me nuts." He dropped the passenger seat forward to let Heidi climb in, then straightened the seat and dropped onto it. "Let's go see if they need help."

Heidi shook her head. "She can be very persistent."

Seth crawled into the backseat from my side and groaned. "Man, Zoe. This back's so tiny for a big guy like me. I'm freakin' sore from yesterday."

Heidi giggled. "Not so tough now, eh? Yesterday you said it didn't hurt." She shifted and made a gagging face. "Ick. What's that smell?" She swallowed and pointed to the front dash. "That air freshener tastes like rotten fruit to me. Can you throw it out? Pretty, pretty please?"

I sat down, fastened my seatbelt, and glanced at my two friends in the backseat. One teeny tiny fairy and the other a distant relative to the Hulk.

Seth plugged his nose. "Why'd you have to mention it?" It came out all-nasal. "Now the smell's overpowering me." His shoulders rose and he swallowed back a gag.

I laughed, reached down, and pulled the pink and red strawberry scented little freshener off my fan vent and tossed it in the garbage can in front of my car. I started the engine. "I'd give anything to block out a sound – any sound."

Brent's eyebrows went up. "It's too much?"

Before I could answer, Seth leaned forward. "Last night's still lingering a bit. If I inhale deeply I can still smell the fire." He stuck his tongue out a few times as if his throat had been scorched.

Brent rolled his eyes. "Dude, I was asking Zoe."

Seth dropped back against the seat, making the whole car shake. "I sense that now." He chuckled. "Get it? *Sense* that now? I totally didn't mean to say that."

"You're a funny man." Heidi voice came across, clear and sarcastic.

"Are you wishing it would go away?" Brent watched me intently and made a conscious effort to speak quietly.

"I don't hate it," I said to Brent as I tried to ignore the cicadas loud buzzing from the trees lining the street and focus on the road. "Look what we did last night." I winked at Brent. "Who'd have guessed we'd be water tower sliding like death-defying crazy tightrope walkers, and then stopping a fire!"

"It was pretty crazy." He grinned. "I'm not complaining about our new skills."

"I just wish they came with an on and off switch." I rubbed my left eye.

"That would be nice." Heidi giggled. "I'd even settle for a dimmer button."

We turned into Brent's driveway and headed around to the gym. Kieran's motorbike sat next to the entrance so I parked the Bug beside it. Everyone climbed out of the car and stretched. As we walked toward the doors I tried to stifle back a yawn.

Brent paused at the door, his hand resting on the handle. "You know what I just realized? Seth and Heidi have similar abilities. Kinda like Rylee and me." He shot me a sympathetic look. "I think it's different for Zoe… Like living with the volume on full blast with everything. You're sort of on your own."

Seth shrugged. "Guess so. Zoe's tough. She can handle it. Kieran should try and help you. Since he's got nothing, maybe he could take up some of the slack." He pointed at Brent. "What've you figured out with your ability? You're skills seem all jacked up?"

"Not really. I think I've kinda figured them out. It's a weird sense of touch ability, but it's not like there's some manual to compare or refer to. My hands are like see-through windows. I touch a wall and can see the other side. I play a guitar and it's like I own its strings."

"X-ray vision." Heidi tapped a finger against her chin. "Which is weird. It's like you've got sight inside your touch. Like two abilities in one."

Seth laughed. "At least if something happens to Rylee, we've still got all the senses covered."

Heidi punched in him the arm.

"Ow! What w—"

"Not funny." Heidi glared at him.

"At all," I added.

Brent tried unsuccessfully to hold back a grin. "Rylee's got super vision. I don't have that. I can just see through stuff with my hands... and my feet. They work too."

"Gross!" Heidi covered her mouth as if the mere thought might give her the taste of feet inside her mouth.

As if to remind me how little control I had, crickets increased their leg rubbing screech, electrical wires hovered like a swarm of bees, and any other little distraction became something big.

Brent opened the door. "Let's go and see what Rylee and Kieran are up to."

The hallway inside appeared dimmed compared to the bright sunlight. Brent's dad had offices and other rooms adjacent to the gym, so barely any sunlight filtered through the hallway. By the time we reached the short distance to the gymnasium doors, my eyes had adjusted. Music blared out of the stereo, making it feel like my eyelids were bouncing to the beat. Kieran and Rylee had been busy. They had rigged part of the equipment so it looked like an obstacle course. Rylee stood on the far side, setting gym mats on the floor so the Velcro lined up. Closer to us, and slightly hidden so I'd missed him on my first sweep of the gym, Kieran lay on his back tying something under an Olympic-sized trampoline. He crawled out when he saw us.

"Oiy! What do ya think? Still need to do that whole section, but it's coming." He pointed to an area with just a ladder with things lying on each rung.

Seth walked over and slapped him on the back. "Great idea. What do you want me to do?"

Kieran pulled a sheet of paper out of his back pocket and showed the hand-drawn diagram which amazingly resembled the gym. "What if we made a sparring area over on the mats Rylee's setting out? This way we've got a bunch of spots and don't need to change it up for a while. I was thinking of setting the ladder up and hanging stuff on it that we would use as stuff to spar with."

"Time out. Time out." Heidi made a T with her hands. "I'm game for setting the gym up, but I can't stay late and NO going outdoors. We need to lay low at night."

"I need to be home too. Loads of homework or my mom's gonna kill me." Seth held his hands out like he was holding a huge weight of books.

Heidi tsked. "Will your dad call our parents about last night?"

"He won't." Seth shook his head. "We talked this morning and he promised not to say anything. I told him you girls were shook up from being trapped in the mine and scared from that night at PHP. He agreed to keep it quiet." He chuckled. "Yeah, my dad's pretty cool."

"Thank goodness." Heidi smiled. She viewed the room and then snapped her fingers. "You know what? We should build some plyometric boxes over there." She pointed to a bare spot in the gym. "To do plyo training. My old gymnast coach was a huge fan of jumping up and over stuff."

"Great idea." Kieran nodded.

Something metal clattered together and fell by Rylee. "Sounds like someone needs some help." Seth winked and jogged away while I covered my ears with my hands.

"We've got wooden crates in storage we could use for the plyos." Brent elbowed Heidi. "Come with me to grab a cart. You can show me how to set them up." They headed to the far end of the gym by the brightly painted orange door.

With my baby fingers I rubbed circles on the sides of my temples. My ears hurt from all the noise, especially the reverberating pounding of the bass coming from the music.

Kieran's gaze travelled from me to the stereo. "Crap! I forgot. Sorry." He jumped up and shut the music off.

For a split second, there was peace and quiet. Then the rest of the world resumed its uproar in my ears.

Kieran shrugged. "I tried."

"Thanks, I appreciate it." I hated the mixed vibes my body kept sending me. One minute it seemed like I was on a one-way street, and the next Kieran seemed to be thinking the same thing. Shame I sucked at flirting. Needing a distraction from my thoughts and something to deafen the noise, I nodded to where Kieran had been working when we walked in. "Anything I can help you with?"

He held a screwdriver in his hand and tapped it against the open palm of his other. "I've been tryin' to think of ways ta help you train yer ears."

I nodded, loving the way his "r's" rolled when he spoke. *Focus, Zoe. Focus.*

"... an' I figured working with yer core balance would probably help everything. Seth made a good point yesterday 'bout that." He pointed to the place where he'd been under when we'd walked in. "I jimmied stuff around the trampoline kinda like a gladiator maze. Trap doors and everything." He scratched his hair near the nape of his neck. "Do ya wan' ta try it tomorrow?"

"Might have to wait a couple of days." I raised my arm and pointed at my elbow. "Don't want to rip this open."

"Oye!" Kieran gently brushed his fingers along the rim of the bruise. "That's gotta hurt." He leaned in closer. "It looks like the scabs starting to come off."

"I ripped it?" I twisted my arm, his fingers still grazing my bicep. It hadn't come loose, it actually had peeled away because it was healing. Weird. The bruise still hurt, but the surface was healing incredibly fast. I wanted to see it closer on my own before I mentioned it to the others.

My face red, either from embarrassment or his touch, I glanced away from his piercing blue eyes. "It's fine. I should probably bandage it. Except my dad's always nagging about scabs needing air, except it'll be gross if I ripped it off."

"Brent!" Kieran shouted, cupping his hands around his mouth to avoid shouting near my ears. "Do you have a first aid kit?"

"In the drawer below the stereo. Everything okay?" Brent called back.

"Yeah, we're good." Kieran winked at me. "Let me find something in the kit to protect that."

Shy but totally loving the attention, I let Kieran rub ointment and then bandage my elbow. I couldn't speak, and thank goodness he didn't try to make conversation either. I didn't want to think except my brain wouldn't listen. It kept wondering if Rylee had talked him into asking her out or, if they'd already tried a thing or two under the bleachers. The thought made my face burn and I avoided looking at Kieran.

"Does it hurt?" Kieran's warm hand gently held my forearm. "Did I make the bandage too tight?"

Our eyes met and I couldn't look away. His brows pushed together with a small crease line forming between them. His handsome face with those piercing blue eyes sent butterflies into my stomach. If he liked Rylee, I was heading into huge disappointment. I shifted my stare to the square patterns on the wood floor. "I'm f—fi—" I cleared my throat. "It's fine."

His grip tightened like a vice on my arm. "What's wrong?"

Chapter 3

Mortified, I blinked and tried not to focus on his strong, thudding heartbeat. "Pardon?!" Was I that transparent with my... my... jealousy at Rylee? I wished the ground would open and swallow me up. Could this be any more freakin' embarrassing? I rubbed my forehead with my free hand. "Everything's loud and distracting. It's impossible to tune stuff out. I can't concentrate," I lied. More like a white lie, as it was true, but my weird actions weren't based on my ears. My lack of concentration had more to do with his proximity.

Kieran quickly let go of my arm, as if he hadn't realized he'd even been squeezing it. His heart rate stuttered at a crazy pace. "Sorry. I just thought... you..." He blew a short breath out. "I got pretty carried away with designing the stuff in here and..." He stopped talking and smiled, his face brightening. "Doesn't matter. I'm sorry you're having a hard time."

"Me too." My face burned. "I'm sure it's going to get better."

Rylee walked over with Seth not far behind. "We're done. I'm ready to head home. Heidi said we have a test in bio tomorrow and I'm totally screwed."

Seth stood, intently staring at his arms as he flexed them.

When he began poking at his chest, I scratched my head. "What are you doing?"

He didn't answer immediately, instead he pulled his shirt off and flexed his chest, his stomach, and turned around to show us his back.

Rylee rolled his eyes. "We all know how built you are, Seth. We don't need the show."

Heidi and Brent stopped moving the crates and boxes and stared at Seth.

"Can't you see it?" Seth raised his arms and with tightened fists he pulled his elbows toward his body. His stomach rippled like there were ten or twelve abs, plus all the clefts and dips at the sides. "We've barely done any training and I'm getting stronger. It's the same for you guys, too."

Rylee laughed. "Whatever. Brent's not even close to your size."

Seth's face didn't change its expression. "I'm serious. I saw it on Zoe last night going down the water tower. Her shirt was blowing and her abs are tight." He swatted Kieran's shoulder. "Tell me you didn't see it."

Kieran grinned. "I didn't see her abs before last night so I've got nothing to compare to."

I ran my hand over my stomach. "It's no different."

"Impressive then." Kieran's grin grew into a smile.

I blushed. *One point for me.*

"Take your shirt off, Zoe." Seth waved Brent and Heidi over.

"I'm not taking my shirt off!" If he asked Rylee, I'd kill him.

"I don't need to see your tiny titties. I want to see your abs."

My cheeks burned hotter. I was going to kill him.

"Fine, whatever." Seth shook his head. "Women," he said to Kieran before turning back to me. "Just check the mirror when you shower later. All of you look. You'll see I'm right. It's like we've been training for months."

"If I promise to look later, can we go home now?" Heidi walked over and stretched. "I'm sore and hungry."

Nobody argued, not even Seth. "Fine. Let's train again tomorrow."

"Zoe, can I get a ride back with you?" Rylee grabbed her backpack by the door and slung it over her shoulder.

"Sure." I suddenly grew giddy. Apparently Kieran hadn't offered to drive her home. "You get shotgun."

We began training every day, spending early mornings in the gym and then trying stuff outside in the afternoon. After a week, I still had a hard time adjusting to my keen sense of hearing. Sounds and resonating reactions like the one from the metal pole were fascinating to try and figure out. The others had the same thing with their senses. Seth had also been right about our physical appearances. All of us were getting stronger. Even Kieran joked that all the equipment moving and setting up was giving him a weight workout.

It wasn't all easy. Muscles I never knew existed screamed in protest. Tendons and ligaments felt like someone had taken a microscopic pair of scissors and cut tiny strands in all of them. Everything ached... and everything healed faster than normal, but it still hurt. The biggest problem was trying to sleep with the world's biggest speakers. They gave me no rest, or the much-needed sleep my body was begging for.

"Did you finish your homework last night?" Mom stopped me in the hall as I came out of the bathroom.

Moms know stuff, like some inner radar, and even though she didn't know what had happened the night of the storm, or what we were doing, she *knew* something was up.

"It's done." I'd gotten up early to have a very hot bath and still felt achy. We'd all agreed to having a morning off. I stood in the middle of the hallway, a towel wrapped around my body and one around my head. I didn't mean to sound snappy; I just wanted to go to my room. Peace and quiet didn't exist in my world anymore.

"What's going on?" Lines appeared on her forehead. "I hope all this exercise isn't for some boy. Are you eating enough?" She leaned against the wall, flicking the hall light on with her shoulder. "You're not turning anorexic, are you?"

I groaned. "Gimme a break. I'm not –"

"You're getting awfully skinny."

"Muscle weighs more than fat, Mom. It takes less space on my body. I'm trying to get lean." Great. Now I sounded like a smart-ass to my own mother! I ran a hand across the towel over my stomach. The mirror had given me a good glimpse of the six-pack showing up on my tummy, with all those little muscles on the sides by my ribs that I'd only seen on guys. Kieran had mentioned core balance might help settle my ears so I'd been trying to do anything that involved ab strength and balance.

"I don't need the attitude." She sighed and dropped her voice. "I'm not trying to nag you."

My shoulders dropped. "I know. I'm sorry."

"Sweetie, you know I worry simply because I love you. One day you'll be a mother and you'll understand why we act so overly concerned."

She wasn't being preachy. She meant what she said. Which made me feel like more of a jerk. "I love you, too. I'm just tired. I haven't been sleeping so great lately."

"Has this been since school started?" I couldn't lie, not to my mom. When I nodded, she added, "Maybe something weird happened that night, down in the mine." She headed into the kitchen. "Your father said he ran blood work on you. I'm going to call him. The results should've been in by now."

"He'd have called us if something was off." *Flippin' brilliant. Now I'd have Dad all paranoid too.* The beeps from the numbers being pressed into the phone was my mom's reply. I trudged to my room, stuck my iPod into the docking station, and flipped it on. Even with the volume set at one, it screamed in my ears. Dropping the towel wrapped around my hair, I paused in the middle of the room. A small *urrr* sound pulsed steadily in the room, about every ten seconds. One hand scrunching my hair and the other on my hip, I tried to figure out where the sound originated.

"Found you!" The noise came from the red light flashing on my blackberry resting on my desk. I had a message.

Two, actually. Hitting the button, I scrolled down to see what I'd missed during my soak in the tub. Rylee cc'ed everyone to remind us we weren't changing the gym around this morning. The second message came from a new email address: themightyscot@...

My chest constricted. I set the phone down and threw on a tank top. I paced the room, hyped up for no apparent reason. Pulling a pair of jeans on, I told myself to relax.

Taking the phone to the bed, I sat down on the edge and hit the read button.

COOL TRAINING LAST NIGHT. WANT 2 GRAB SOMETHING TO EAT AFTER SCHOOL 2-DAY? BEFORE WE HEAD BACK TO BOOT CAMP BASE. K—

I jumped off the bed and ran as hard as I could on the spot. I'd have screamed "ahheee," but didn't want my mom to barge in. Tired? Who's tired?

I needed a super-cool reply.

FOOD SOUNDS AWESOME. WE MIGHT HAVE TO BRING SNACKS BACK FOR SETH AND BRENT. IF THEY SMELL FOOD ON ME, THEY'LL CHEW ME OUT FOR NOT SHARING ☒ BCB (BOOT CAMP BASE) – PERFECT NAME BTW... Zzzz

I ran by to my closet. What the heck should I wear today?

Kieran stood leaning against my locker after the last buzzer. The blue from the old lockers made his eyes appear even brighter. Dark hair, grey polo, and jeans with a slight tear in the knee, could he get any hotter? He seemed oblivious to the girls walking by him, saying hi and giggling when he nodded in their directions. Squaring my shoulders, I tucked a chunky strand of hair behind my ear and made my way over.

"Hu-llo, Zoezey."

That accent's going to be the death of me. I loved the way he used my dad's nickname. Nobody else used it, but from him it sounded... good. I fumbled with my locker combination.

It was impossible to miss what the girls around me where whispering.

What's the new guy doing with **her***?*

Does Rylee know she's got some competition?

Don't worry, he's probably kissing up to get calculus answers.

It took everything inside me not to turn around and say I could hear them. I knew I stood no chance against Rylee. If Kieran liked her, I knew what would happen. And that'd be okay. I'd be alright with it. I scoffed. Really? I don't think so!

"Let's get out of here," Kieran said, picking up my backpack off the floor and slipping it over his shoulder. We passed Brent and Seth on our way out.

Brent glanced back and forth between Kieran and me, his mouth hanging slightly open. "Y-You heading to the gym already?"

"Shortly," Kieran said. "Just popping out to get some tea."

Seth snorted. "Tea? Like a cup of it?"

Kieran's eyebrows rose, but he didn't smile.

Brent elbowed Seth and said, "He means they're grabbing dinner."

Seth's lips made a circle shape. "Whatever." He made a smooching face behind Kieran's back at me, then dashed to Brent's car before I could throw something at him.

"See you in a bit." Brent's gaze lingered on me. Doing a half turn, he turned back and said, "I meant to ask you, I wrote a new tune and need your opinion. Want to stop by later and let me know what you think?"

I felt Kieran stiffen beside me and his breath sucked in sharply. "I'd love to, but I can't tonight. I should head home after the gym. My mom's getting paranoid." I hated the disappointment in his eyes. We'd always hung out. "Why don't I come by on Saturday?"

"Perfect." Brent smiled, running his thumbs along his finger pads. I'd noticed he fidgeted with his fingers a lot now. It had to have something to do with his ability to see things through them.

"Cheers, mate," Kieran said as we headed toward the Bug. "Hey, would you mind if I tried driving?" He flashed me a smile that looked half embarrassed. "I 'aven't driven a car since coming over. Only me bike. Yers is... well, it's small and safe..."

I grinned and tossed him the keys. "And not shiny and new."

He opened the driver's side door as I jumped into the passenger seat.

"Don't you think to lock yer doors?" he asked.

"Have you seen the outside of this thing? Anyone desperate enough to try and steal the change out of my cup holder deserves to have it."

I giggled when he forced himself into the driver's seat. As he sat, his knees pressed between the steering wheel and the dashboard. He tried reaching between his legs to get the handle on the bottom of the seat to slide it back. His elbow got wedged against the wheel. He looked at me and grinned. "It seems I'm in a bit of a pickle."

"Pretzel, definitely not a pickle." I laughed. "Need some help?"

"Not quite as flattering as I pictured this would go." He shook his head, but chuckled.

I leaned forward, inhaling husky male cologne which made me instinctively close my eyes. My hearing perked up a notch, noticing the quickening on Kieran's heartbeat, which sent mine in a frenzy of its own. Holding my breath I reached down, letting my arms and ribs brush against his hard leg. The tips of my fingers felt the cool plastic of the release button, and gave it a gentle tug. Except the pressure of Kieran's knees against the dashboard and steering wheel sent the seat flying backwards.

I lost my balance and went flying with him. My head landed on his lap. *Smooth move, Zoe. Head right between his legs.* Face burning, I used his knee to prop myself up. My head ended up inches away from his. For the weirdest moment, nothing made a sound, like we were frozen in time. I could see little flecks of aqua green inside his blue eyes. From this close, they were breathtaking.

He smiled, and as I inhaled slowly, a peppermint scent drifted by. I held my breath, unable to breathe. Noise filtered back into my ears and crashed against the inside my head. I dropped my gaze from his eyes to his mouth and impulsively I pressed my lips together. His smile faded and he swallowed hard.

A horn honked somewhere and I jumped. The moment was over. I inhaled and disappointment filled my lungs as I sat back against my seat. *Stupid sonar hearing.*

"Th-Thanks," Kieran said and cleared his throat. Popping the clutch, he turned the key and revved the engine once it started. For a guy who'd never driven a car on the right side of the road, he had no problem. The Bug never purred this nicely when I drove. I sighed. Guess she liked him too.

"Crap!" Kieran muttered.

"Something wrong?"

"Yeah. Well, not really." He paused, then forced air through his nostrils. "Do you mind if we swing by my place for a moment?" His fingers tapped against the steering wheel. "I forgot my wallet."

"I can pay."

"Uh-uh. I'll just run in and grab it. Won't take a sec. My dad's working, so no one's home."

"Sure." I relaxed a bit more. *He's kinda nervous too.*

We drove in silence and I stared out the window, blinking when we pulled into his driveway. Small, old windows, and made of wood, his place looked more like a cabin than a house. The gravel driveway seemed to have more weeds than pebble on it. I caught sight of the back end of his motorbike sticking partly out behind a rickety old shed.

"I know. It's a crap-hole." Kieran parked the Bug.

"I never said..." My voice trailed off. "It's... it's not so bad."

"Sure, maybe a hundred years ago. I'll be right back." He was out of the Bug before I could respond.

I settled against the seat to wait. The overgrown grass made me think of my dad's place and how he took such pride in keeping the lawns immaculate, his and my mom's.

Just as Kieran unlocked the front door, I heard noise from inside. Glass clinking against a glass, the sound of ice cubes cracking as warm liquid tried to break them. Heavy, slurred breathing and someone stumbling from the rear of the house toward the front, banging into furniture, and something being knocked over.

"Someone's broke in," I whispered. My hand grabbed my seatbelt and I unclicked it as my other hand reached for the door handle. I jumped out of the car to warn Kieran.

I didn't need to.

Kieran's body went rigid. "Insolent bastard. I let me guard down for one moment..." He swore under his breath but I heard him clearly. He huffed, then turned to me. "I'll only be a moment." He stepped inside.

Even if I tried, I couldn't have missed the conversion inside the house.

"Yer 'ome!" A male voice shouted in an accent stronger than Kieran's. It sounded like an accusation.

"Iye. So arr you." Kieran's accent thickened to match.

Hearing the tension in the air, I slowly made my way toward the house. I didn't really want to go inside but wasn't about to leave Kieran on his own. He hadn't been doing any of the training, nor did he have a hidden talent.

I peered inside the front window.

The entrance had an old, built-in, half bookcase which overlooked into a living room with worn furniture, walls in dire need of paint, a coffee table with three legs – a stack of books as the fourth leg – and an old, rabbit-ear TV. Amidst the mess, an older, bigger, and slightly dirtier version of Kieran was sprawled on the couch, drink in hand. Struggling, he got to his feet, spilling amber liquid over his hand and onto the floor. He didn't seem to notice.

"Miss work agin, Da'? Or you get fired?" Kieran accused.

"Shut up, boy." His father's voice shook with anger. "You tryin' to pick er fight?" He brought his arm toward Kieran, showing the backside of his hand. "I'll knock you on yer arse, again."

No wonder he didn't want to come by here or have me come inside. My hearing ability would be useless in protecting Kieran, but maybe if I walked in the house, his dad would put on a show and act polite. I swallowed hard and raced up the steps before I lost my nerve. I flinched when the wooden screen door slammed behind me.

Kieran glanced at me but did not move. "I left me wallet. We'll be outta here in a sec."

I panicked. *Should I have waited outside?* My eyes darted from him over to his dad and then they automatically flew to the front door.

"Who'z this?" His dad's tone changed instantly to a freaky-friendly one, and he dropped his raised hand. "You bringing a cute lass to the 'ouse?" He set the drink down and stumbled toward me. "Welcome ... Wha'z yer name, sweetie?"

"Her name's Zoe," Kieran snapped. "And we're in a rush. I'll introduce you to her another time... when you're... feeling better." He reached for my hand and pulled me into the hall. Out of the corner of my eye, I caught sight of the kitchen. Where the living room had been a mess, the kitchen appeared neat and tidy. *Almost spotless.* Only an empty bottle of whiskey sat on the counter.

I followed Kieran down to the end of the hall. He paused by a closed door. I pointed, unable to stop myself from blurting, "There's a lock!"

A large silver lock hung on the doorframe with a latch screwed into the door. Kieran stood quiet, his heart switching to an erratic rhythm. "My father sometimes thinks its fer me own good."

Horrified, I wondered what kind of life he'd lived and how he kept it hidden so no one could tell. I'd have never guessed. *Poor guy.*

"Don't look at me like that." He pushed the door open. "The ol' man doesn't know I have a lock on the inside to keep him out, and a window 'bout three feet above the ground. Not quite that hard to git out. I'm usually on me own." He grinned. "An' don't worry, he won't come in my room."

Tentative, I glanced down the hall and heard steady breathing. Focussing a little harder, I could tell Kieran's dad was breathing through his mouth. A small amount of phlegm gave the sound a gurgle kind of snore as he inhaled. *Eww!* How did someone go from threatening to beat your son, to sleeping like a baby that quickly? I didn't feel the need to ask. Instead, I quickly stepped into the room.

Neat, tidy, and organized – like the kitchen. His room had a double bed, the sheets made military style, a bookcase with half the shelves empty, and a tall dresser with each drawer closed perfectly.

My eyes locked onto the single item on top of the dresser. An amazing crystal flower. A Scottish thistle. *Wow. Totally stunning.* The sunlight sparkle through the window caught each cut of crystal and cast a million rainbows across the walls. "That's beautiful." I walked toward it, passing Kieran who had his back to me while he rummaged through his closet.

"Just need a sweatshirt. It feels like it's gonna git cold tonight and I need an extra top if I'm on me bike." The last half of his words were muffled as he stuck his head further into the closet. My hearing easily picked everything up.

Standing in front of the thistle, I shifted slightly left and right, fascinated by the rainbow of colors. I couldn't tell if the purple on the thistle was amethyst or lighter, it seemed a million different shades of one colour.

I wonder if the crystal's cool to the touch... it seems like it might be warm...

"Don't touch—" Kieran fumbled as he turned away from the closet, knocking things off their hangers in the process. I jumped, startled, my hand midair. My hip knocked against the corner of the dresser and Kieran tore the few steps to get beside me. He reached and steadied the wobbling flower.

"It's Waterford. One of a kind. Extremely expensive."

"I'm sorry." I wanted to disappear, my hand flying to my mouth. My face burned. "I didn't mean—"

"I know." He swallowed, putting his hands on my shoulders and moving me back a step. "It was my mother's. It's the only thing I have of hers."

Now I felt even worse.

"Don't worry. It's fine." He pointed at the flower. "See? Nothing wrong, she's safe. I didn't mean to scare you." He checked his watch. "We should go. We aren't going to have much time before we 'ave to meet everyone at Brent's." Taking my hand in his, and grabbing a green sweatshirt off the floor as we passed the fallen pile, he led me down the hall. He stopped by the front door and reached around the back and pulled out a leather coat.

The living room now sat empty. *Where'd his dad go?*

"I'm going to take my bike. So you don't have to drop me off later."

My heart dropped into my stomach. "I-It's not a big deal. I don't mind bringing you back."

He smiled. "Thanks, but I'm gonna need a long ride later tonight." He played with the fringe on his jacket sleeve. "It's going to cool down, so if you don't mind taking me jacket in yer Bug?"

"Sure." As I opened the front door, a chilly gust of wind blew in. I shivered and glanced back at him, eyebrows raised. I laughed. "You do that?"

Chapter 4

Brent

Typical for Friday night, Pool Hall Parlour's live music did not disappoint. The in-house band consisted of a piano player, who sang, and a guy with an acoustic guitar. They actually weren't half bad. If I had my bass, I'd have asked to do a few songs with them. It'd be interesting to see how the fingers played with my skills now.

"Dude. Can you listen for ten minutes?" Seth peered from behind an open newspaper held high in his hands. He made the paper snap, then folded it and tossed it onto the table. "Nothing. Absolutely-friggin'-nothing."

I waved as Zoe, Rylee, and Heidi came in through the front door. All three with damp hair. *Probably showered after messing around with our abilities by the train tracks.* Tapping my fingers against the table, I let the mental picture of the three of them showering together—

"Are you ignoring me again?" Seth pounded my fingers.

"Hey, watch it." I rubbed my hands protectively. I waggled my fingers. "I need these babies. They're my instruments of power now." I laughed at his confused expression. "Okay, so what's up?"

"I've gone through four papers from the surrounding areas. There's nothing worth chasing. No serials killers, rapists, bank robbers... nothing. We can't solve any crimes or stop any bad asses worth risking our lives for."

"Or worth getting our little secret caught over?" Zoe teased as she slid in the booth beside me. She grinned and shrugged. "Sorry, I heard you from over there."

Thank goodness you can't read my thoughts as well.

Seth sighed. "How're we gonna save the day, if there's nothing going on?"

Rylee dropped beside him. "Don't say that. Now, you-know-what's going to hit the fan, and a whole bunch of crap's going to start happening."

Heidi laughed as she squeezed in beside Zoe who, in turn, moved closer to me. She smelled of soap.

"Ryls, when'd you become superstitious?" Heidi asked.

I glanced back at the entrance. "Didn't Kieran come with you guys?" I avoided looking at Zoe.

"We dropped him off a bit ago. He wanted to get his bike," Heidi said. She grabbed a menu. "I'm starving. Have you ordered?"

"We waited for you." Seeing the disappointed look on her face, I added, "But we did order the leaning-tower-of-rings."

Kieran needed his bike? He'd left with them in Zoe's Bug. Maybe he wasn't interested in her, just needed a lift home. I scoffed. Fat chance of that.

"You okay?" Zoe stared at me, a little wrinkle forming between her eyebrows.

"What?" I drummed my fingers against the table again. This time I got visions of the floor and our feet, and then Zoe's face. In my nervousness, I kept switching my skill off and on. Clasping my hands into tight fists, I slipped them under the table.

"You snorted," she said, "like you were pissed off, or something."

She knew me too well. "Nothing. Band's just playing a good song. I should've brought my guitar."

Seth gave a look, as if to say "Idiot." Then his gaze drifted past me to someone behind us.

I didn't need to have eyes in the back of my head to know Kieran had just arrived.

Zoe heard him come in. She straightened, tucked a curly lock of hair behind her ear, and grabbed lip gloss out of her bag. I wish I could put my fingers against her scalp and see inside her brain. *Duh, maybe I don't want to know.*

"Oye! Sorry I'm l-late." Kieran held his bike helmet under one arm. His chest heaved in and out, like he'd been running, even his leather jacket appeared rumpled. He took a deep breath and ran a hand through his hair. It took him three tries to hang the helmet on hooks attached to the side of the booth. He settled beside Rylee. "'Ave you ordered?"

Abi came by with two leaning stacks of onion rings. "On the house."

"These smell awesome." Seth leaned over, past the onion rings and sniffed. He gave Abi his best flirty smile. I kicked him under the table. "Ow!"

Abi took our orders and headed off to the kitchen. Seth watched her, then glared at me. "What the hell was that for?"

"Dude, she's like twenty-one and was almost gang-raped."

"Too soon?"

"Wayyyyy too soon."

Rylee giggled. "Find someone your own age." She looked meaningfully at Kieran.

"Where'd you go after we finished?" I asked Kieran. Part of me wanted Rylee to shut up, the other part wanted her to score with the guy—just so Zoe'd lose interest.

Kieran stared at me in silence, before finally answering, "Home... and a bike ride."

"It's freezing out." Rylee squeezed closer to him. "Why in the world would you want to do that?"

Kieran didn't say another word for a long moment, only let his eyes shift over us. "Me dad's gone."

"What?" Zoe shot forward on her seat, grabbing Kieran's wrist.

"Ouch!" Kieran pulled his arm away. He coughed and covered his mouth. His sleeve slipped down, revealing a huge welt with four long, jagged cuts. I could see swelling and even the start of some serious bruising.

"Oh, my goodness. What happened?" Zoe had gone pale and her eyes were huge.

"N-Nothing. Must've done it at the tracks." Kieran pulled his sleeve down, looking a little too intently at the menu. "Me dad's gone to Scotland. Said he needed to see some mates and take care of some business back 'ome."

"How long's he gone?" Seth butt in, ignorant of everything that had just passed, except the parent-free house. "Party at your place."

"Uh... okay." Kieran shrugged. "But I live in a shite-hole. We're better off hanging out in Brent's gym." He turned to me, his eyes almost begging me to say yes. "What say you, Sight-man?"

I wanted to hate the guy, but Zoe told me about his place, and his dad. My dad was lame, but given the nasty mark on his arm, his won hands-down. Plus, partying in the gym would piss my dad off. "Why not?"

"Then crash at Kieran's after," Rylee said, resting her head on his shoulder.

Heidi laughed. "All of us? Or just you?"

Rylee's mouth dropped open in surprise but she didn't blush.

I stared at Heidi in surprise but also didn't miss someone else snort. Heidi never dissed Rylee. She never dissed anyone. That was more a Seth comment. I glanced at Zoe from the corner of my eye. She sat picking her fingernails, pretending to be oblivious to the conversation but I knew she was listening to every word, sound and then some more stuff none of us could hear. She could probably hear someone's heartbeat changing or their temperature rising.

"There's a bunch of rooms at the back of the gym," I said, trying to steer the conversation in a different direction before claws started coming out. "We could bring sleeping bags and camp out in there." I ran a finger over the pattern on a napkin. "Shoot, there's a hyperbaric chamber, as well."

"A what?" Zoe's eyebrows went up then dropped as if it took too much effort.

Poor thing, she looked so tired.

"Hyperbaric chamber," Heidi explained. "It's a specially equipped pressure vessel used to administer oxygen at elevated pressures."

"Ohhh..." Zoe nodded, but her face showed she didn't understand.

"Yeah that, and it looks pretty cool. Like a submarine." I grinned. "Dad bought one of the double chambers. He said he wanted the extra space. I've been in it a couple of times. Half an hour in there, and your head clears all the fog out." A thought struck me. I nudged Zoe's shoulder. "You need to try it. It's pressurized, so it mutes most outside noises." I tried unsuccessfully to not look down. Her already hot body was turning rock-hard – but the smudged purple under her eyes wouldn't disappear.

"Sounds awesome. I'm at a point where I'll sleep under a rock if it'd help." She squeezed my knee and mouthed, *Thanks.*

"Instead of a party, how 'bout we just hang out? With the six of us." Heidi tapped her spoon against the table. Five taps later, Zoe gently rested her hand on top of hers and the tinging noise stopped. "Sorry." Heidi smiled at her apologetically. "Too many people and I start tasting everyone. I know it sounds weird but I don't know how else to explain it. Someone's going to start stinking and I swear I can taste it. Or some idiots are going to start smoking pot." She made an ick face.

"I'm actually with you on that," Seth leaned forward. "Not the pot smoking, but everything smells too sweet, too salty, and too awful. I can handle the six of us." He smiled, and patted Rylee's back. "You guys don't stink."

"Ta... I think." Kieran pretended to sniff the air. "I'm in for the hanging out night. When are we going ta do it?"

Everyone turned to me. "Saturday?" I offered. My folks would have some function they had to go to. Plus no school.

Seth clapped his hands. "I'll bring a crap-load of newspapers to go through. Maybe we can head out before and find something to do. Practice saving someone or something else totally cool."

"I think looking for something is going ta be like waiting fer a pot ta boil." Kieran scratched the back of his neck. "Leave 'er be and something'll come."

Seth groaned. "Wait? We've been waiting for like a month. We need to find or make our own action. Otherwise it's never gonna happen." He turned to me. "I'll bring papers, and maybe some walkie-talkies. I'll steal my little brother's. He's got like three pairs of those superhero comic ones."

"Aye. I'll be your Alfred." Kieran laughed.

Bastard. Even his laughter had an accent. "Our what?"

"Batman's behind the scenes guy. I'll be your driver, the video guy, or whatever else."

Seth leaned over Rylee and high-fived Kieran. "That's awesome. 'Cept you ride a bike. We need other wheels, and the Bug ain't gonna fit all of us."

"I can get my mom's station wagon," Heidi offered.

We all laughed. "Not quite the superhero vehicle I pictured." Seth chuckled. "But it'll have to do."

Saturday, after clearing the large meeting room, stacking tables and chairs against a wall, I dropped into a large leather computer chair and surveyed our handiwork. With Kieran, Rylee, and Heidi's help, we'd carried some of the gym mats into the room so we could sleep on them. Dad had a large flat screen mounted on the wall for computer presentations so I'd taken my laptop, cords, and one of my speakers so we had some good surround sound. There was a mini fridge and microwave behind the door and Mom insisted on having sandwiches made and about a hundred mini bags of chips with other snacks set out on the table. There was enough food to feed an army.

The only sour touch to the afternoon was Dad mumbling about having a teen-orgy on his property. Thank goodness Mom hadn't been around to hear my response.

Seth marched into the room, carrying a stack of newspapers. He dropped them onto the table right by where Rylee and Heidi had set their feet on. "What's with using Christmas lights to mark a path in the hallway?"

"My idea." Rylee tapped her chest. "I figured it looked more like a cinema."

Kieran pushed himself into a sitting position from where he lay on the floor. "This place is big enough to have its own theatre."

"Where's Zoe?" Seth glanced around and poked his head out the hall.

"Not here yet," I answered.

"Doesn't matter." Seth waved a hand. He walked back to the pile of papers. "I've found something we can do. A crime." He stood, looking all pleased with himself.

Heidi grabbed the top paper and began scanning the cover.

"It's not in any of these. I heard it on the radio on my way over." Seth rested his back against the table, crossing his arms. "Who knew those A-M channels would be useful one day?"

"What is it?" Kieran leaned forward, resting his elbows on his knees.

"A-M. They're radio stations that have sports or talk shows and stuff."

"No, I meant what's the 'crime'?" Kieran said.

Seth paused, looking at each of us before answering, "A mysterious dead body. Right. Here. In Elliot Lake."

I straightened, shocked. "Murder?"

Heidi and Rylee gasped. Even Kieran looked uncomfortable.

"Not sure exactly. Radio just said a body'd been found in the ditches near the mine. We need to investigate and solve it ourselves." Seth began pacing. "If it's some serial killer, we could stop it. And find out if anyone else is in danger."

Rylee stood and grabbed her coat. "Let's get going."

Heidi walked to the fridge. "We're not going straight to the crime scene. It'll all be taped off. We'll have to wait in the car or sneak around the area and see if we can find clues or hear something." She began throwing wrapped sandwiches in her bag. "Might be a bit of a wait. No sense in getting hungry while we're there."

"You mean, you guys really want to go?" I couldn't believe what I was hearing. *But hell yeah!* It'd be cool trying to figure out what the cops were saying, use our little talents and... the challenge of not getting caught. It was too hard to resist. I bent down to tie my runners. "Let's go catch us some criminals."

"Wait a minute," Kieran said. His hands were clenched, the white of his knuckles bright against the blue mats. "Where is Zoe?"

Chapter 5

Zoe

"Zoe, you are not leaving until we talk."

I had my back to Dad, but knew he stood leaning against the wall with his arms crossed. He seldom raised his voice, instead, it would become hard and he'd enunciate every syllable and sound. Sighing, I stopped putting my coat on and turned to face him.

"Why don't we sit in my office?" His voice softened, but he had his practitioner look.

Crap. I'm already late meetin' up with everyone. My stupid fault, not Dad's. I shook my head. Arguing would only make me later, and the whole reason I wanted to spend the weekend here was so I wouldn't have to explain to Mom about sleeping at Brent's. Not sure if Dad knew the whole truth if I'd be in any less trouble.

I tossed my coat on the front closet doorknob and led the way down the hall to the first room. It'd originally been a third bedroom, now turned into Dad's office. I flipped the light switch and the pot lights flickered on. Like the rest of the house, simple beige colored the walls but the doctor feel of the room stared bleakly at me. The mahogany desk sat under the window and on each side; against the wall were large antique bookcases full of med books so thick the side writing looked like a Latin alphabet.

Dad followed and walked behind the desk. He pulled a file out of his briefcase and set down on his brown leather chair. Hands folded, he tapped his thumb pads against each other as he waited for me to sit down.

"Alrightie, I get the hint." I snuck a peek at my watch, already twenty minutes late—not counting drive time. "What do you want to talk about?"

He hesitated and I knew immediately the file was mine. The blood in my veins went from ten to a hundred miles an hour. What could be inside? Could he know about me? About all of us?

"Your mother's worried," he began.

I grinned, despite my nervousness. "She's *always* worried."

"Zoezey." The concern in his voice stopped me from saying another joking comment. "You've lost weight. You look like you haven't had a good night's sleep in weeks." He opened the file, sifting through the pages till he found the one he wanted.

"I'm *not* anorexic. I've been working out." A twinge inside warned me not to be too defensive. "The entire gang is. Seth made up this exercise routine, and challenged us all."

He stared at me with his doctor's eyes, but said nothing. He had obviously come to the conclusion that I'd changed since the incident at the mine.

"My bed at Mom's sucks so I'm sleeping crappy." Lame. Really lame.

He sighed. "I've got your blood work results."

I didn't like the unreadable look on his face. "And?"

He cleared his throat. "Things were... off."

Oh shit.

He slipped his reading glasses on and glanced down, reading off some list. "You're low on iron. Your WBC count is way up, and you haven't had a cold or been fighting any infection."

White blood cells? What teenage kid cared? "Dad, I'm fine... more than fine." Should I tell him? Tempted, I paused when I heard him blink several times, heard his heart start racing, and realized he was scared. That flew up warning flares I didn't like. What had him so worried? I swallowed, trying to wet my dry mouth. "What's up?"

He rubbed his face. "There's trace amounts of uranium in your system. It's not much, but any amount isn't really good." He flipped to another page. "And, oddly, some carbon. I ran some different kind of tests... ones I sort of invented at my lab. It appears as if uranium has attached to your red blood cells, but in a complex mitochondria – in a weird way. Not like I've ever seen before." He reached his hand out and realized I sat too far away to touch me. He dropped his arm but began talking again, moving his hands for emphasis. "I've told no one and there's no reason to be alarmed. I'd just like to run some more tests. It's probably nothing... but you know me, I like to worry."

"Okay..." I didn't get the whole mitochondria thing, but didn't want to ask tonight.

"Have you noticed anything out of the ordinary? In any of you?"

He liked inventing tests or looking for weird things in results. Anything to challenge his incredibly smart brain. His heart rate raced again. He was getting excited now, too.

What should I say? Tell him the truth or wait? "Nothing's weird." I had no right to tell him about the others unless they agreed to it.

"Can you, and maybe Heidi or Brent, come by my clinic this week?" He cleared his throat. "I'd rather err on the side of caution."

My head tilted slightly and I tucked a lock of hair behind my ear. Liar. His entire body shouted it to me. There was more he wasn't saying. Hadn't Heidi said uranium caused cancer? I didn't want to be a bald seventeen-year-old spending the next three years in a hospital. Should I ask Brent? If we all had it, Brent's dad would probably build a hospital in the name of research to save his son. Not that he cared if he saved Brent, it'd just look good in the papers. Not fair to Brent. Heidi would have a heart attack if I asked her. *Kieran*. He was the only one without a talent. Nothing would show up in his blood work. Hopefully Dr. Dad would lay off then or starting thinking mine would start clearing up. Especially since I wasn't getting sick.

Dad swivelled in his chair and grabbed the med bag on the shelf behind him.

"Uh-uh." I stood and waved my hands in front of me. "You're not doing blood work tonight." I started for the door. "I'm already running late. You can drain all of it tomorrow. I promise. Later, Dad." I left the room and jogged down the hall before he could argue.

I grabbed my keys off the hall table and swung the front door open, about to race out expecting Dad to coming down the hall, needle in hand.

A large bulky shadow, their hand in a fist, blocked my exit.

Jumping back in surprise I squared my shoulders ready to scream. My ears zoned in and picked up on everything going on inside and outside the house.

All of it in like a second: heavy breathing at the front door, Dad opening his laptop inside his office, then another sound crystal clear—Rylee, Kieran, and Brent laughing inside Heidi's car. "Seth!"

"Did I scare you?" He chuckled. "I was just about to knock. I figured you'd hear us from miles away. We got tired of waiting."

I pushed past him. "Let's go." If Dad started talking to Seth, he'd get him in the clinic tomorrow.

"Bye, Mr. Taylor," Seth shouted as he slammed the door.

I jumped, my feet literally leaving the ground.

Seth reached out to steady me. "My bad, again."

Stepping off the porch, I caught the sound of Seth's erratic heartbeat, and his body swaying. He was excited. It wasn't like him to stay quiet and not spill the beans. I doubted I'd have to wait long.

Halfway down the drive, he started whispering, "We got something to solve. Something big." He bounced while he walked. "Police found a body." He glanced back at the house, making sure my dad wasn't outside. "We're going to check it out."

We'd reached the station wagon. Brent jumped out the back to let me in and Seth climbed into the front, squeezing Rylee between him and Kieran, who sat behind the steering wheel. Kieran driving?

"I'm Alfred, the chauffeur," he explained as if reading my thoughts.

I sat beside Heidi, with Brent now on my other side. "Dead body? Where?" Kieran pulled away from the curb. The radio was on some news station, tuned quietly but blaring in my ears. By the loud buzz, it was A-M radio.

"By the mine." Seth put his arm around Rylee and turned back to look at me. "I heard it on the radio. Some guy was walking his dog and found it."

I'm not going near that mine. I shuddered and tried shifting in my seat to hide it. "The cops aren't going to let us just walk up and have a look." My gaze slid over to Heidi. She'd have already brought up this argument.

"We're going to park far away and see what we can figure out." Heidi made a circle with her finger, pointing at all of us. "You'll be able to hear what the cops are saying, and Rylee can see from far away, et cetera. Test out our skills in a real situation."

"Wee bit o' fun tonigh'," Kieran chuckled. It sounded forced.

"Oh... okay." I glanced at the back of his head and tried to see his face in the rear view mirror. Only hair and a bit of forehead was visible.

"I wonder if it's murder." Seth leaned over Rylee and started flipping through the radio channels.

Rylee swatted his hand and took over, finding some eighties music station. "Only old people die in Elliot Lake."

"Or snowmobile accidents in the winter," Heidi added.

"Let's hope it's no one we know," Brent said quietly, his face serious.

That shut everybody up. We drove the rest of the way in silence, listening to a song end and then the local weather forecast.

"Where d'ya want me to go?" Kieran turned onto the long road which led to the mine. He seemed to be getting to know the area pretty well now. Probably driving on his bike to avoid his deadbeat dad.

Seth pointed to the right. "There's a gravel road leading to the wooded area by the mine about fifty meters from here. How about we go as far as the road'll let us and then get out and walk through the forest."

I glanced at Heidi and Brent. Both wore jeans, black tops, and runners. Looking down at my yellow hoodie, Converse bling sparkled across the front and flashed like a neon light. In my rush to get out of the house, I'd left my coat. "Guys, I'm not dressed right."

Kieran glanced in the rear-view mirror. "Me jacket's black and I'm wearing a dark grey sweater underneath. I'll give you me top when we pull over."

Brent grunted beside me.

"Thanks." I envisioned him taking his top off in slow motion, no tee shirt underneath, just hard, taut abs and sexy body. I blinked when Kieran cleared his throat and brought the car to a crawl.

He cut the engine and we sat in silence, looking out the front window. The forest stood dark, but red and blue lights flashed on top of the trees and bounced off the clouds.

Cocking my head, I tuned in to try and hear what the cops were saying. I closed my eyes, trying to eliminate the physical noises of the five sitting close to me. Straining, I could just make it out.

Coroner's on the way. Ten minute e-t-a.

Don't recognize the body.

Only way we're gonna get an ID is through dental records. The guy's head's smashed in pretty bad. The animals have done a number as well.

I grimaced, wishing now I could block out their voices. A shivering chill slithered up my spine like a slippery snake. "It's definitely murder." I told them what I'd heard.

Quietly, we all slipped out of the car. Kieran stood by the opened driver's side door and took off his jacket. He pulled his head out of his hoodie, revealing a tight, Under Armor white top. "Here, Zoe." He handed the sweater to me.

The warmth of his skin lingered as I slipped it on, his smell filling my nostrils, tempting me to close my eyes.

"Let's just go through the forest, but not get too close," Brent said. He stepped between Kieran and me, and handed each of us a flashlight. "Don't turn these on unless it's an emergency."

"Good thinking." Seth flipped his light on to see if it worked and then off again. "Rylee, you lead the way."

"Wh-what?" she squeaked.

"I'm right behind you. Don't worry." Seth patted her butt. "We just need your eyes." He stuffed his light into the front pocket of his jeans. "And don't be reaching back, pretending to grab my flashlight. We *all* know you can see."

"Not even I can see good enough to find what you want me to grab." Rylee smirked. "You're sad."

"Pathetic's a better word," Brent said. "Zoe, you go behind Seth so you can listen. Tell us if it's anything good. I'll go behind you, then Heidi, and Kieran can bring up the rear."

Everyone started on the gravel road toward the trees, except Kieran. He seemed reluctant. I jogged over to him standing by the car. "You can wait here in the car if you prefer. You don't have to come."

He looked surprised, then smiled. Bending low to whisper in my ear, his hot breath sent prickles down my neck. "Ta for yer concern. 'Tis nothing. I just need to have a wee chat with Mother Nature."

"Pardon?" I glanced at the gang now waiting for us twenty meters ahead.

"I need ta piss." He pointed to some shrubs by the car.

"Oh!" I could feel the burn on my cheeks. "I'll, uh, wait for you over there then." I dashed back to the group. Why did I have to embarrass myself around him all the time?

Kieran, now wearing his black coat, caught up just as the gravel road ended and a path led into the forest. Dog owners usually parked in this area so the worn path created a shortcut to the large open field on the other side.

As we walked, Rylee seemed to be the only one not stepping on twigs or dried, fallen leaves or anything noisy and squishy. After ten minutes of hiking, she slowed and held a hand up.

I listened. No need to strain, I could hear everything. The frustrating part was getting it all at once, not zoning out certain sounds like Brent breathing beside me, Kieran humming a tune, and Heidi's nervous teeth grating. By the mine, another automobile had driven to where the cops were. It was some kind of heavy, slow vehicle. Maybe an ambulance... or the coroner.

"I can see a bit between the trees." Rylee stood on the tips of her toes, a hand over her eyes as if shielding an invisible bright sun. "The body's covered with a sheet and there's like a dozen cops. The area's roped off with yellow 'caution' tape. The flashing lights, and a beam from above is throwing my sight off." She rubbed her head. "I'm getting a headache."

What too much sound was to me, probably felt like constant strobe lights to Rylee. I felt bad for her. "Let's see if I can hear anything." I closed my eyes and plugged my nose trying to just focus on listening, no other sense.

Never seen anything like this in Elliot Lake. And I've been on the force near thirty years.

This is going to shock the entire county. I hope it isn't the start of some serial killer. I can't imagine this escalating much more.

This was a serious rage crime.

The policemen stopped talking when someone walked by. Plastic crinkled in an awkward way. Probably the tarp covering the body being lifted.

Oh my... followed by the gross sound of someone throwing up.

Rigor's set in. The guy's solid. Decomp is pretty advanced. Body's been here five, maybe ten days.

Five or Ten? That's a big gap.

It's been cold a few nights, below freezing, so that slows down decomp. I won't be able to give you more information until I get the body to the lab. Shuffling and more plastic wrinkling and scrunching, followed by a zipping noise. *I hope there's one useable finger to get a print. It looks like some of the fingers were burned, then the frost and nature seems to have done the rest.*

I repeated everything I heard in a whispered voice. My mind shot horror-film images flashes in front of me as I listened to the police talk. I needed a breather. Raising my arm on a nearby tree, I buried my face into the crook of my arm. With my free hand, I pressed my fingers into my temple and closed my eyes to rub them. Pressure at the back of my head seemed to be working its way around the front.

Trying not to hear, I couldn't block out any of the noises. They wouldn't stop. *Like a bad dream you can't wake up from.* I heard Kieran move toward me before I opened my eyes.

"Hey, you okay?" he whispered. He put his hands on my shoulders and pulled me close. It felt awesome to have my back pressed against his warm chest. I shivered and it had nothing to do with being cold, and his near proximity made me tingle. I hoped no one could pick up on it with their sonar sense. He had rock hard abs, just as I'd imagined.

Brent grunted as he put a hand on an ancient oak and, using his other hand, took his sneakers and socks off.

"What're you doing?" Seth waved a hand in front of his face. "Your feet reek."

"I want to see if I can get sight off the ground. I thought if I tried burying my toes into the dirt, I might be able to see more. My skill's all whacked and while you guys are all struggling to get yours, I think mine's come too easy. There's got to be something more to it."

Seth started complaining again but Brent held up his hand. "Give me a moment, I'm actually getting something."

"What?" I leaned forward to get a better look. Kieran's long arms stayed around my waist.

Brent closed his eyes. "I'm following the dirt path to the field. The body's on a gurney now... looks like they pulled it from a shallow ditch or some kind of dry ravine." His eyes flickered back and forth across the back of his lids. "I can't see the body." His eyes snapped open. "Rylee, did you get a chance to see it?"

"No."

Except her face had turned four shades of green and I could tell her stuttering heart and churning stomach said the exact opposite. Obviously something we don't need to see. I tried to swallow. This was way too intense.

Seth coughed. "All I smell is your stinkin' feet and the shit-stench of a dead body." He gagged. "It's going to take a week to get that smell out of my nose hairs."

Everyone started laughing. Only Seth.

Giggling, Heidi covered her mouth. "I have to breathe through my nose, and keep my lips closed tight. If I get a taste, you'll be adding puke to the already horrific smells."

Smiling, I opened my mouth to add something funny but stopped when Kieran stiffened against me, his arms tightening and pulling me closer. I looked up at his face. He cleared his throat and stepped back, his arms leaving coolness as they left their embrace.

"We should git outta here. If we keep laughin' the cops mightn' hear us."

Brent walked back and bent to collect his socks and shoes. "I'm with the Scot on heading back. My toes are freezing."

Rylee's breath sucked in. "A couple of flashlights just shone into the forest in our direction—"

"Yeah," I interrupted, my own heart rate picking up. "Someone heard us. They're heading to their cars to grab some more lights."

"Run!" Seth hissed, grabbing Rylee's hand and pulling her. "Get back to the wagon as fast as you can."

Chapter 6

"I'm not spending the night in jail." Heidi gripped the back of the driver's seat as the rest of us clamoured inside the car.

Kieran tore out of the gravel side road. Tires squealed in protest when they hit the paved street. Sitting in the middle of the backseat, I slammed into Brent and then bounced against Heidi as the vehicle straightened. The distance between us and the mine couldn't be far enough for me.

"We're not going to get caught," Kieran said, his voice tense.

"Even if we do, we won't get arrested," Seth added. "Cops'll just give us a warning about how irresponsible teenagers we are, and how we won't grow up to be participating members in our society."

Brent grinned. "Been there before, buddy?"

Seth glanced at us in the backseat. "Couple of times." He turned back around when the car veered sharply as Kieran swerved around a bend in the road. "Go down the next street on the right. It'll take us to Brent's place. Few more stop signs, but hardly any street lights. Good ol' country roads. Lots big, old trees."

Five rolling stops later, Rylee started giggling.

"That *was* pretty awesome." Seth nodded. Even Kieran, whose knuckles were white from holding so tightly to the steering wheel, smiled.

Brent pounded the car's ceiling with his fist, and shouted, "Can I get a holler?"

Heidi and I screamed, "Whoop! Whoop!" Then we dissolved into laughter.

"Seriously though, that was pretty crazy." I said as we neared Brent's place.

"We need to plan this shit out better." Seth punched his knee.

"Yeah, like not go." Rylee sighed, shaking her head. "I was so stressed. I think I just took ten years off my life. Or way worse. I'll probably be dead by the end of the year."

"Hey, dead-dude's got no stress now," Seth joked. No one laughed. "Too soon?"

Brent leaned against his seatbelt and swatted the back of Seth's head. "Yeah."

"Whatever." Seth rubbed his head. "You know what we need? Outfits. I'm gonna look online tomorrow. Maybe I can find something on eBay."

Rylee snapped her fingers. "I'll look. No way am I letting you choose what we wear. I can only imagine what you want to get for Zoe, Heidi, and me."

Seth grinned. "Yeah, you wouldn't like it. But you'd be totally hot." He leaned away from Rylee's fist, easily missing it. "We'll look together. I don't trust you either."

Kieran pulled the car alongside the gym, mere feet from the doors. He put it in park and handed the keys back to Heidi.

We piled out of the car. Brent unlocked the gym and then slipped inside. By the beeping of buttons, I heard him turn off the alarm. Funny, each key made a slightly different noise, like a telephone. It wouldn't be difficult to figure out a combination if I listened hard enough. After tonight, avoiding any cop situation might be a better idea.

"It's getting cold out," Rylee murmured, her breath sending puffs of smoke into the air.

Brent leaned out the door. "It's off. We'd better get into our sleeping bags before someone finds out where we were."

"Sounds good to me." I slipped under his arm and inside. Relaxing and trying to sleep would be a lot better than talking about the lonely, cold, lifeless body. I shivered, not liking the mental picture.

In silence we set the gymnastic mats on the floor with our sleeping bags over top. Rylee, Heidi, and I slipped into another room to change.

"Rylee," Heidi asked, "Are you okay? You're awful quiet."

Rylee sighed. "I just wish I could get the image of that poor guy's body out of my head. It's so freakin' crystal clear." She rubbed her eyes. "This sense-thing is a blessing and a curse."

Heidi hugged her. "I brought hot chocolate. Let's go make some."

When we got back to the room, the guys were eating chips and popcorn. I couldn't resist teasing Seth. "I thought you said the smell at the mine wouldn't leave your nose hairs for weeks. A bag of chips and a whole bowl of popcorn for just you? Seems your appetite is back."

He grinned and tossed a few popped kernels into his mouth. "Seems the butter managed to remind my gut what's good for it."

Kieran sat at the table doing a crossword from one of the newspapers. "So what do you guys think? Will you guys be able to find out what happened at the mine?"

"I don't know." Brent came out from the bathroom connected to the room. "It's not like we know more than what the cops said. They'll do an autopsy and it's not like we want to break in and see what it says." He dropped down on the couch and stole some of Seth's popcorn. "From what was left of the body, the guy was probably homeless or something."

Seth shifted and turned just as Brent leaned over to grab another handful. "I'm not giving up. I bet we can find out who the guy is – was before the cops." He pointed a greasy buttered finger at Brent "And figure out who killed him."

Rylee, now standing behind Kieran and looking over his shoulder at the crossword, took the hot chocolate Heidi offered. "I agree with Seth. If I gotta live with that image in my head, I want to know who it is."

Heidi slipped into her sleeping bag. "Can we just give it a rest tonight? I'd rather not get caught by the cops and wait till the papers or news say something." She yawned, a big long one which got me then everyone else copying.

Shortly after, each of us crawled into our makeshift beds. No one felt like trying to make conversation, we must have each been lost in our take of the evening. One by one they began nodding off.

An hour later I shifted, trying to find a comfortable spot on the floor. The ground felt too hard, my sleeping bag too tight. The sounds in the room were overly annoying. I'd finally started getting used to the night noises at Dad's and Mom's houses. Here, everything drove me crazy. Seth's lumberjack snoring, Rylee's moan every time she exhaled, Brent's constant finger drumming against the gym mat, Heidi sounded relaxed, which made me jealous, and then there was Kieran. His erratic breathing and changing heart rate kept me from dozing.

Sighing, I rolled over and exasperatedly kicked at the bottom of the sleeping bag, trying to free my tangled feet.

"Can't sleep?"

I nearly bolted when Kieran's whisper shouted in my ear. Across from me, he sat slightly sideways, his lower body covered. The room was dimly lit by the full moon through the window. His pale, lean torso rippled against his ribs and taut muscles stretched across his back and down his arm. The eerie blue night light seemed to gravitate toward him. Not that I could blame it.

"Everything's kinda... noisy." I leaned on my elbows and shrugged.

He unzipped his sleeping bag and crawled out. "Come on." He tiptoed over and offered me his hand.

I slipped mine into his warm, calloused one and let him pull me up. We grabbed our gear and snuck out. We could've driven a garbage truck through the room. Those guys weren't going to wake up for anyone or anything.

"Where're we going?"

"The room a wee further down the way." His accent sent tantalizing shivers down my spine. "Brent said his dad had a hyperbaric thingy-medoby."

"Chamber," I corrected, feeling a little nervous, though not sure why.

"I think it's gonna help you, maybe dampen the noise."

He turned the knob on the second to last door, and flipped the light switch.

I blinked, trying to adjust to the sudden brightness and looked around the room. I started laughing when I saw the chamber. It looked like a submarine, except Brent's dad had painted it like a Canadian flag. All bright red and white enamel.

"'e's a bit patriotic?" Kieran raised his eyebrows. "Me dad've painted it like a kilt. Maybe a bottle Bovril." He blinked and swallowed, his face suddenly serious. "It's big."

"Yeah, Brent's dad does everything that way. There's a hyperbaric bed at the hospital by my dad's office and it looks like a giant baby incubator. It's see through on the top. This one's probably got a launch pad somewhere and it'll shoot off into space."

Kieran walked around the room, and opened a door to a closet. "No launch pad in that." He headed over to the controls and hit a few buttons. Clicking, swooshing, and a loud pressure release squeal sounded. "Thar pretty easy to use. Just need to set the timer." He played with a few more dials.

The door to the chamber had one of those handles that reminded me of a submarine. I wondered if it had a steering wheel doorknob on the inside. Walking over, I poked my head through the doorway.

Two single beds with pillows and sheets sat on each side, and also a small writing desk. I dropped my sleeping bag on top of the thin sheet and turned to check the back of the door. Kieran ducked his head as he came in and held the door. The knob was a push bar.

"It can't lock us in," he said. "You needn't worry, lass." He let the door click shut.

I smiled, about to reply, when the quietness of the room dispelled all train of thought. I heard our hearts beating, semi-steady rhythms, and Kieran swallowing before he set his sleeping bag on the other bed and sat down. He looked questioningly at me, his face so hopeful.

Like a knight in shining armour. "This is really nice." My voice seemed to echo against the walls, so I dropped it to a whisper. "It's awesome." Without thinking, I leaned over and hugged him. "Thanks."

He smelled musky and heavenly. My nose, or maybe it was my body, begged me to inhale again and memorize the scent. His arms came around my waist, his hands resting on the small of my back. I dropped my head to his shoulder. It fit perfectly.

"Hey," he whispered, leaning slightly back.

I lifted my head and looked into his steel grey-blue eyes. They flittered back and forth between mine, then dropped down to my mouth. I felt his heartbeat hammering as mine raced alongside. He brought his head forward and I closed my eyes, letting my lips open a little. His were so soft. It was a light kiss. Slowly I opened my eyes to see him staring at me.

Weird, I'd only kissed a few guys, and they'd never kept their eyes open. I wondered why Kieran did.

Looking sheepish, he grinned. "You're so pretty... I wanted to make sure I wasn't dreaming."

He probably said that to every girl he'd ever kissed, but telling me those words, I believed him. I blushed, he had spoken like he'd read my thoughts. "I think maybe this chamber's filling up with something other than oxygen." *Bad, bad, bad joke.*

"Whatever the drug, or gas, I like it." He bent toward me again, this time closing his eyes. The kiss deepened and I loved the feeling of him pulling me tight. Too soon, he moved his hands to my sides and gently pushed me back. "I'd love to do this all night, but I didn't bring you here for this. I am a bit of a gentleman. At least I try to be. You need sleep. And I need to take you out on a proper date before I kiss you."

Sigh. Big movie star sigh.

He slid off the cot and made my bed. "Git in and I'll zip you up."

His moisture still on my lips, I pressed them together for a moment. "You don't have to take me out on a date to kiss me. Honest, I don't mind." Instant burning to my face. Could I sound more trampy? I blinked when a horrible thought crossed my mind. Maybe there was something wrong with the way I locked-lips.

He kissed my forehead. "I dig you. You're the first good thing to walk into my life in a long time. I don't want to screw it up."

Ahhh... my insides melted. If he asked me to rob a bank with him, I'd do it. Fly to moon? We could use this hyperbaric chamber and turn it into a rocket. Funny, maybe every girl had these silly fairy tale thoughts.

Kieran squeezed behind his cot and pushed it a bit closer to mine, and then went over to shut the lights off. The little round windows kept the room bright from the fixtures outside the chamber.

"We forgot –" I started.

"Remote." He held up his hand, holding a tiny, black, TV-looking remote. Pressing a button, the room went instantly dark. I heard him slip into his sleeping bag and settle on his back, his hands behind his head.

I thought about his lips against mine and tried to focus on something – anything – else. "I'm not tired now."

Kieran laughed. "Me, either."

I said the first thing that popped into my head. "Have you heard from your dad?"

"Me dad?" I heard his fingers scratch against his scalp. "He's, uh, good."

Poor Kieran. Apparently he hadn't patched things up. How awful. I couldn't imagine fighting with my dad that long. "When's he coming back?"

"I dunno know." He paused. "Maybe in a couple of months."

I pushed up on an elbow. "A couple of months? He just leaves you on your own? What about groceries? Bills? Money to pay for everything?"

He lay silent and I scolded myself for being so nosey. It wasn't any of my business.

"It's not a big deal." Kieran shrugged, I heard his shoulders crack and relax against the sleeping bag. "He sent me money yesterday actually. And I usually do the groceries anyway."

"I can make a mean bowl of spaghetti and meatballs. I can come over and make it a night if you'd like. Or, you could come to my place." I cringed. He'd probably zoom away on his bike so fast after being interrogated by my mom or dad. Either house we were screwed. "You know, kinda like a date."

"I'd like that." He yawned, long and deep. "Hmmm... let's talk in the morning, 'eh?"

"Sure." I listened to his heart settle into a slow, steady rhythm, his quiet breathing music to my ears.

It felt like moments, but when I rolled over and checked my watch, I was startled to see the clock read after seven a.m. The silence inside the chamber reminded me where I'd slept, and who lay in the cot beside me. I sat up and stared at Kieran.

His long, lean body stretched out on top of his sleeping bag, his ankles crossed and an arm thrown across his forehead, covering his eyes.

I stared at his face, seeing a slight trace of dark stubble. It tempted me to run my knuckles light over it, to check if felt smooth or like sandpaper. Looking down, I shoved my hands under the blanket, less they decide to have a mind of their own.

Glancing up, I noticed a slight smile on his lips.

"I'm awake," he said. "Don't drill me wit' a pillow." He moved his arm and looked at me, resting his chin in his palm. "It's pretty quiet in here for you, right?"

I nodded, part of my brain wondering how he could look so hot first thing in the morning. This only made me think I probably looked like a rumpled shirt. Pulling my band out of my hair, I redid my pony, then changed my mind and stuffed it into a bun.

"I was hoping it would work. Maybe the extra oxygen in here will do something good for your ears. Like take some extra crap out." He pointed to the door. "Can you hear anything from there?"

The flashing buttons made a little clicking noise. Easy to detect. "Yeah, but—"

He pointed to his feet and wiggled them. "Can you hear them?"

I listened, letting the clicking noise fade out and noticed his toes crackling as the bones slid against each other.

"What about the lights? Is there a buzz from the electricity?"

I glanced up and heard the sound... for the first time since I'd woken. "How'd you do –"

"I didn't do anything." He grinned. "I just had a gut feeling the hyperbaric chamber might help muffle out some of the noise... make it like a background sound. I hoped it might help you control, like zoning in and out."

"Way. Too. Cool." I jumped off the bed and stretched my arms toward the low ceiling. "I believe I owe you my sanity."

"Darn." He snapped his fingers dramatically. "I'm a little particular to the insane."

I grinned. "Spend a year in Elliot Lake. The boredom will make you crazy."

"Since coming, I don't believe there's been a moment of dull."

"True." I needed to pee. Not exactly something you want to share with a guy you're crushing on. "We should probably check if the others are up." I headed for the door. "Best sleep I've had in a long time." Looking back, I watched Kieran grab both sleeping bags, haphazardly rolling them up. An idea struck me. "Hey, my dad wants me to do some blood work. You know, to make sure there's no radium in it. He asked me to see if one of you guys would do it also?" I shrugged. "Since everyone's folks are home and'll get paranoid, would you come?"

Kieran stopped rolling the bags and stood quiet for a moment.

"You don't have to," I said, trying to make it sound like no big deal. "I just figured... your dad's away and your blood's probably the cleanest of all of us..." I let my voice trail off and chewed the inside of my lip, waiting for him to say something.

He picked up the sleeping bags. "Is this your way of getting me to meet your da'?"

My mouth dropped, probably into a perfectly circled 'O'. I hadn't even thought of that.

He winked. "How 'bout Thursday or Friday? Maybe you can make some of that spaghetti bolognaise you were talking about afterwards?"

Play it cool, girl. "Sounds perfect. It'll get my dad off my back." I reached for the door handle. "Now I wanna see if I can make the noises driving me crazy become background when we're outside of here." A huff escaped my lips. "I doubt it's going to work."

He smirked. "'Ow, much you want to bet?"

Chapter 7

The night in the chamber changed everything.

My perception of sound became, in a way, controllable. I could focus on the noises I wanted to hear, and shove the other sounds into the background. It took a couple of days, but by Monday I was able to centre myself and listen – or *not* listen.

Whatever happened inside the chamber enabled my brain to muffle all the annoying: like electricity running, the wind howling, people shouting when they were only whispering. Somehow the extra oxygen or whatever else cooled the over-firing synapses with my hearing. Or something along those lines as Heidi explained when I'd asked her. I could zoom in when I wanted to and tune out when I needed to. The best part – I could sleep. Only once in a while I'd wake when a strange sound startled me.

Sleep became a dream, no longer a nightmare. Amazing how letting the body rest made everything so much better... and clearer. Hard to believe a few nights of decent kip felt like three months to my body. *Heavenly.*

"Space-case... Yo, Zoe. Are you going walk the beam or just keep standing there staring into la-la land?"

Seth's teasing brought me back to the present. Barefoot, I spun on my right foot, which had less balance than my left, and ran across the beam to finish with an ariel. I landed on the mat in a perfect gymnastic finish. "Ta da." I stuck my tongue out at him.

"Show off." He winked at me. "It's about time. I was wondering when the girl from the water tower planned on coming back."

"What's that supposed to mean?" I jumped back on the beam to try and do a handstand. Balance seemed so incredibly easy now, I craved to challenge it.

"Don't take this wrong or get all girl-mad on me but..." he stared as I held the handstand and watched him upside down. "Zoe, can you flip over? I've never looked at you as more than a little sister but your shirt's showing off a rockin' body that's distracting."

I started laughing and lost my balance. My feet fell backwards but instead of wiping out or breaking my neck, I turned in the air to land on my knees and hands just in time.

Seth ran around the beam to see if I'd hurt myself. "You're like some freaky cat."

"Thanks." I stood and pulled my shirt straight. "Now, what were you saying before I distracted you?"

A confused look crossed his face before the light bulb went on. "Oh yeah. After the mine you seemed you but you also seemed kinda cocky." He held his hands out in front of him when I crossed my arms over my chest. "I mean that in a good way. Like, confident. You seemed confident. And daring. Which is totally cool." He nodded his head. "You kicked Brent's ass at the water tower—"

"I heard that," Brent called from the plyo boxes and walked over. "She barely beat me."

I laughed. "Ha! I kicked your butt."

Brent rolled his eyes. "Barely, and if I hadn't given you that head start..."

"Whatever!" Seth and I said at the same time.

"Anyways," Seth continued, "You were all tough and daring and then the mouse came back and you went all timid."

"I'm not timid."

Brent put his arm around my shoulders and gave me a squeeze. "I think Seth means tired. You look great now." He dropped his arm and stepped back. He cleared his throat. "Is that what you mean, Seth?"

"Yeah, something like that." Seth looked around the gym. "Dude, I can't believe how much money your dad has. This place is unbelievable. My dad would be yelling to put the all the toys away every night."

Brent shrugged. "He comes in the place, but I doubt he ever looks in the gym."

I didn't say anything but I could tell Brent didn't want to talk about his dad, or his money or stuff like that. He hated it.

Seth didn't get it though. "How much money does your dad make? It's got to be in the millions."

"I've no idea." Brent started walking to the punching bag.

Seth followed a step behind him. "He's gotta be doing stuff under the table, like cash deals. I bet he hides it, buries it in the yard somewhere or hidden deposit boxes all over the place."

Brent didn't answer. He began hitting the punching bag with a sort of vengeance.

I couldn't help but overhear their conversation and figured Brent was imagining Seth's face on the bag.

"He's paying for your university education, right? No way the rest of us are going to get that easy ride. Except maybe Zoe. Her dad's loaded as well. Not like yours, but he's *the* doc." Seth held the bag so Brent could punch it harder. "I bet your dad's pissed you're into music."

Brent stopped punching. He held his arms at his sides, clenching and unclenching his fists. "Seth, I'm only going to say this once. Shut up. Or I'm going to use you as my punching bag!" His face burned red and his lips pressed into a thin, tight line.

Kieran brushed my shoulder as he passed by and marched over to Seth and Brent. "Why don't we give this a rest? Call it a day, shall we?"

Seth glared at Brent. "Fine. I'm outta here." He turned to go and then spun back around to Brent. "You've got it made. You have all the money, all the means to do whatever you want, and of course you then have to get the best ability. You never have to work for anything. It's annoying as hell sometimes." He huffed and stormed out of the gym.

All of us stood, open-mouthed, watching him leave. I heard his car door slam and the stream of swear words fly out of his mouth as he drove off. I'd never seen him act like that before. He was competitive by nature but this wasn't that. He seemed… jealous.

I walked over to Kieran and Brent. So did Heidi and Rylee.

"Ignore him," Heidi said. "He'll be fine tomorrow."

"I hope so," Rylee mumbled.

Kieran shoved his hands into his pockets. "How 'bout we just give 'im some space?"

"Yeah, I could use some myself." Brent grabbed his hoodie and headed out of the gym without looking back.

I hated the frustrated look on his face. Brent never acted like he came from money, and the whole music and university thing was a sore spot between him and his dad. I couldn't believe Seth had brought it up. Part of me was tempted to go after Brent and talk to him. I held back, unsure if he would want me around.

Hopefully whatever had irritated Seth today would be gone by tomorrow.

Chapter 8

"We're going shopping for *costumes*?" I tried not to snort. *Could Rylee really be serious?* I checked my blind spot and changed lanes. "It's impossible to find a good parking spot downtown. We're going to have park at the parking garage and walk to—"

"Block up the road, car just pulling out, and the meter's still got fifty minutes on it," Rylee shouted, or it seemed that way to me. She popped her head forward from the backseat of the Bug. "See that car pulling out just past the lights?"

"Quick, Zoe." Heidi turned to Rylee. "Put your seatbelt on, girl. You're going to get in an accident one day and there'll be nothing there to stop you."

Rylee collapsed against the backseat. "Fine! But hurry, some dude's going to steal it otherwise."

I laughed. "There's no one in front of us, and the car's barely pulled out." I sped up anyway and then had to brake hard to let the humungous old car, with a tiny elderly lady driving, have enough space to pull out. One little tap from that car and my Bug would probably land six streets over. Manoeuvring an easy parallel park, I finished the skill by yanking the parking brake and cutting the engine.

"I'll feed the meter. I've got loads of change." Heidi jumped out of the passenger seat and flipped the back of it over so Rylee could get out. She ran to the front of the Bug and tried to pop open the hood. "It's stuck, Zoe."

Rylee crawled out the backseat. "It better not be. My school bag and purse are in there." The ancient Bug had its trunk in the front and the tiny engine in the back.

"It's locked." I jingled the keys. "No super-hero *or outfits* required."

Rylee rolled her eyes. "We're not going to buy stupid capes or anything like that. Think about it though." She bent forward and grabbed her purse after I'd unlocked and opened the hood. "We need flexible clothes, like when we're training."

"Seth warned me: nothing in hot pink," Heidi called from the meter. "Though he did say he'd like a Superman shirt with an "S" for his name. And as for a cape, he's ok with that." She giggled and swung her purse over her shoulder. "So where are we going?"

I dropped the hood and had to push it hard to get it to click shut. "Which way, Rylee?"

"Maybe Value Village? We can find matching black pants or tights online or at the mall. Something from Under Armor or Nike or whatever, but we need to find some tops."

"Or," I offered, getting a little excited despite my initial hesitation, "we could try the comic book store. The back part's got shirts and paraphernalia."

"Awesome idea! If they've got nothing we like, at least we can brain storm and I'll find the perfect outfit. I'll find what we need." Rylee grabbed both Heidi's and my shoulders and swung us around to walk in the opposite direction. "It's left at the corner and up the block a bit. Shorter than walking to Value Vil—"

SLAM!

Someone raced from around the corner of the building and banged into us. All three of us crashed to the concrete with the boy falling with us, his backpack tumbling and thumping to a stop against our parking meter.

Ignoring the sharp, burning pain on my elbow, I cocked my head to see if I could hear anyone else coming. The grunt and heartbeat of the boy sounded familiar. I couldn't see his face as I'd fallen with my back to him.

All three of our senses must have picked up at the same time. "Kieran!"

"Oye!" He pushed himself to standing and held out an arm to Rylee as Heidi and I sat up. "I'm sorry. I didna' see you." He reached for my hand and helped me up. "You okay?"

"Yeah, just scraped my elbow a bit." I lifted my arm and touched it. Just my luck it was the same elbow that I'd banged at the water tower. Luckily no blood.

He turned to help Heidi. "Why were you running so hard?" she asked.

Kieran glanced behind him and did a full turn. "Where's me bag?" He found it and raced over to grab it.

"What were you running from?" Heidi repeated, louder.

"Running from?" Kieran blinked and then smiled. "No. I saw the Bug drive through the lights an' figured I'd try and catch up with you. Didna realize you were *that* close. I wanted to catch up, not catch you and send you flying. Sorry 'bout that."

Rylee went to stand close to him. Very close. "Oh, did Seth tell you we were going to get some outfits?"

"Outfits?" Kieran asked.

"Costumes," I muttered while Rylee rambled on.

Heidi giggled and nudged me. She licked her lips and a weird look came over her face. "What's up?" I whispered, even though it sounded like a shout to me.

"I just got a weird taste in my mouth. Salty and ick." She licked her lips again and swallowed.

"I've got a water bottle in my bag. I'll go grab it for you." As I walked to the Bug, a loud *ee-unn—ee-unn* noise filled the air. I had to cover my ears from the noise. *Police.* That was probably where Heidi got the bad taste from. Using my shoulder to cover one ear, I popped open the front hood with my free hand and dug into the side of my backpack.

Kieran came beside me. "D'you mind if I put me bag in here as well?" He glanced up and watched two police cars with sirens flashing race by us. "You okay?" He seemed pale.

Cute, he's worried about me.

Rylee slipped her sunglasses on. She'd mentioned the other day that flashing lights bothered her eyes and gave her a headache.

"You okay?" Kieran repeated, his lips close to my ear.

I shivered. "It's like a dog trying to ignore a dog whistle being blown inches from him. Toss your bag in. Did Rylee rope you into coming with us?" Spotting the water bottle, I grabbed it and leaned behind Kieran and tossed it to Heidi. "The bad taste is probably from them," I said to Heidi, nodding my head back toward the direction the cruisers had raced.

Kieran tossed his bag into the Bug and it landed with a clunk. "Here, let me get that for you." His hands covered mine as he reached to close the hood. "Ow. Your elbow looks a wee bit rough. You mighten' need a plaster." His finger traced down my forearm but didn't touch the scrape.

"Plaster?" I sounded like a parrot. *Stop staring into his eyes.* I blinked several times but didn't look away. I couldn't think properly when I got lost in their oceans.

"Band-Aid." He corrected and winked at me.

"Oh. I've got some in the glove compartment." *Thanks, Dad, I owe you one.*

"I'll grab you one." He took my hand and led me over to a frowning Rylee and water-guzzling Heidi.

"Can you grab me one as well?" Rylee said. "I've hurt my finger."

"You okay?" I asked.

"I hope so. My nail broke right near the skin." She wiggled her finger close to my face. "It's going to hurt like a son-of-a-gun if I snag it."

Kieran returned with two Band-Aids and administered them to both of us. "So where were you girls going to when I bowled you over?"

"Comic Book Store," Rylee said, linking her arm though his. "I was thinking turquoise tops with some kind of superhero design. What do you think?"

Heidi rolled her eyes and the two of us walked behind Rylee and Kieran. "We need something dark or unassuming. We want to go unnoticed, don't you think?"

Rylee crossed her arms. "I figured it'd be cool to have something blue. You know, like how we were all blue the night in the mine."

Kieran chuckled. "Nice idea. However, I think eventually we're going to git noticed no matter how blue the color is."

"Why not a dark blue?" I thought of Brent and wondered how he was doing. He had acted normal at school today. So had Seth. Maybe they had talked and worked things out? Guys were so complicated to figure out.

"Hmm... with dark blue, I could figure out some fancy design to do on the arm or over the wrist. Maybe we want a long sleeved and short sleeved shirt." Rylee quickened her pace, looping her arm through Kieran's again and pulling him along.

We walked single file into the Comic Book Store, following Rylee's lead. She went straight for the back room and started flipping through the clothes on the racks. Kieran leaned against the back wall, flipping through some comic book while Heidi and I checked the other rack. We had no idea what to look for, trying not to giggle too loud as we held up the ugliest tops we could find. We only showed each other, and Kieran.

"I know what you guys are doing," Rylee warned. She forced a hanger back onto the rack and shook her head. "We need a lightweight, maybe nylon or some kind of stretchy material."

"Like Spiderman's?" Kieran held up the comic he was reading.

Rylee snapped her fingers. "Exactly! That's brilliant."

Heidi's eyes shot my way and she mouthed the word "Brilliant?"

I stifled back a giggle and had to pretend to sniff my nose and look for a Kleenex as I sniffed loudly again to try to cover myself.

"Let's go." Rylee headed for the exit, her head down as she tapped with crazy fingers into her phone. "Can you drop me off first?"

We all followed her lead. "What about costumes?" I asked.

"They're uniforms. Outfits," Rylee corrected. "I've got the perfect thing."

"What is it?" Kieran asked.

Rylee pressed a long, manicured finger over his lips. "Shhh..."

I smiled when Kieran went cross-eyed as he stared down his nose at her finger.

"It's going to be a surprise. I just need to email Seth and Brent to find out their measurements. You guys email me yours as well. Everything, like height, leg length, shoe size, bra size." She clapped her hands and squealed. "This is going to be so awesome!"

I had a feeling it wouldn't be, but held my tongue.

Chapter 9

Thursday after working out I rushed home, changed, and drove to Kieran's. Training had gone well and the tension between Seth and Brent had disappeared. They had definitely worked things out, or had just simply ignored it the typical way only guys could do.

I pulled my dilapidated Bug into his drive. You couldn't miss the fresh cut grass and cleaned off walkway. Pulling the bag of groceries out of the car, I glanced around again. The cabin actually looked like a house now.

The recently swept porch had a new swing set up. The front door was open with only the screen door closed but not locked. I knocked and opened it. Small town, everyone did it. "Hello? Kieran, it's me." I stepped in and looked around. The living room was empty. Sort of.

The place had gone through major transformation since the last time I'd been there. The three-legged table was gone, a new wooden one sat in its place. All the litter and crap covering the floor had been cleared away. Kieran must've polished the floor. It shone like an ice rink. The TV was on, so Kieran had to be around.

I jumped when a thundering filled my ears and crashed around inside my head. Shivering, my fingers pressed instantly to my temples to calm the noise. Down the hall, water began running. *Pipes*. Water pushing through the pipes to the faucet. If I wasn't prepared, surprise noises still shocked me.

Eyes closed, I listened to the sound of a pair of jeans dropping in a hamper and a shower door sliding open. Streaming water splashed against naked skin. Swallowing hard, I slipped into a now spotless kitchen and forced myself to block out the noise. *I'm eavesdropping.* I pulled out the tomato sauce Mom and I had canned over the summer and a bag of noodles, and set them on the counter. The onions, mushrooms, and peppers got stuffed into the fridge, along with the hamburger mince I'd bought. It was too early to start chopping and cooking dinner.

Tossing the paper bag in the bin, I headed back to the living room and settled on the couch. The television had the news on. I grabbed the remote off the coffee table and turned the volume down a few notches. The anchor woman rambled on about the sports scores, a robbery at a betting shop in the county over, and then in the top corner of the TV flashed a body covered in a tarp. The screen flipped to a reporter talking about the John Doe body found at the old mine.

I leaned forward, trying to memorize everything she had to say. Maybe there'd be something worth sharing with the group.

"...nothing more has been determined about the John Doe found last week at the closed down uranium mine in Elliot Lake. Police have been unable to identify the body and are waiting for further testing results to come in. If anyone has any information, police are asking you to call them, or the anonymous tip-line number on the bottom of the screen."

The cops hadn't figured out anything more, and neither had we. Our "talents" obviously weren't that useful.

A click from a door opening had my head turning toward the hallway. Kieran stepped out of the bathroom, a white towel wrapped around his waist. I couldn't stop myself from staring at his long upper body, lean and rippled with taut muscles. His shaggy wet hair dripped water and splayed in every direction. I heard each droplet that splashed against his skin.

I swallowed hard. A yearning inside me begged to know what his hair and body felt like against my fingers... and against my skin. A part of me was tempted to follow him down the hall. Then reality set in, and I almost giggled out loud at the thought of scaring the crap out him and his towel dropping to the floor... I covered my mouth. The tramp inside me needed to take a long holiday... or a cold shower.

Kieran took two strides toward his room and paused. His hand squeezed the knot in the side of his towel. He slowly turned.

"Zoezey. Am I running late?" His brows shot up and tiny, adorable lines creased his forehead.

"N-No. I'm a bit early. The door was open." I tried to keep my eyes on his face, but they kept trying to drift down.

He smiled. "Give me a sec." The hot body disappeared into his bedroom. "Is yer dad's office at the hospital?" Kieran spoke as if I were in the room with him, I could hear him that clearly.

"Yeah. He's got a spot in the wing Brent's dad built a couple of years ago." I spoke, then realized he couldn't hear me so I repeated it, louder.

"Is thar anything he doesn't have his hands into?"

"My dad?"

"No, Brent's." Kieran came out of his room wearing jeans and a black shirt with a Ranger's logo over his heart. "Seems like the guy owns half the town."

"He knows how to make money, and spend it." I shrugged. "He's done good stuff for Elliot Lake. My dad chased after the provincial government and federal for years trying to get a better hospital. They wouldn't budge, so Brent's dad pulled some strings and donated the wing." Under Brent's dad's insistence, Dad had his own lab added for some medical thing he was researching.

"Nice guy." Kieran didn't sound convinced.

I had a hard time arguing, and I wasn't about to bring up fathering when Kieran was obviously happier with his dad gone. Turning the TV off, I got off the couch and walked to the front door. "This shouldn't take long. Just a bit of blood work."

He patted his back pocket. "Do I need me NHS card?"

I looked at him from the corner of my eye, raising my eyebrows.

"Me health card?" He teasingly tugged a strand of my hair.

"I doubt it, but take it just in case." I slipped my hand in his and pulled him outside. It seemed the natural thing to do. He locked the door and as we walked to my car, I tossed him my car keys. "You can drive."

With the parking pass my dad insisted I keep in the glove compartment, Kieran parked the Bug beside my dad's Volvo. He pulled the keys out of the ignition and fiddled with the miniature guitar chain I'd bought on a class trip last year. Brent always joked it was his favorite part of my car.

"So, what's yer da' like?" he asked.

I smiled. Kieran wanted to impress my dad. "He's cool. Worries about me too much, but that's okay. He never remarried after he and my mom split."

"Yer folks not divorced?"

I scratched the back of my neck and stared out the window. "Technically, no. They're separated but that's not even with proper papers. I think both of them have gone on a few dates but, never met the replacement."

"The replacement?"

I turned back to watch him. "When I was, like, thirteen I made the term up. Love was never the problem between them. My mom couldn't handle my dad being married to his work and to her. He'd've done anything she wanted, so he gave her space. I figured they were both looking for *the replacement* and were just too stupid to realize they didn't need one. Wanna know something? I bet that once I go away to university, they'll get back together." I knew they didn't break up because of me, I just hoped they'd realize how much they meant to each other when I wasn't around.

Kieran sat quiet for a moment, apparently digesting what I'd said. Or maybe what I didn't say. His eyes lit up and he grinned.

"You don't seem ta be so great in the bettin' department. Mightinbe best to avoid gambling. At all costs."

I pretended to punch his arm. "Ha. Funny little Scotsman." I glanced at the clock on the car radio. "We'd better go or my dad's going to think I stood him up."

We headed inside and down the slate floor hallway to Dad's office.

A new secretary greeted us. She was about ten years younger than Dad. Pretty, but with a face which seemed to lack any expression or feeling. *Probably ticked she's working late.*

"Dr. Taylor'll be back in about ten minutes," she said, barely glancing up from the file on her desk. "He's just gone up to check on a patient in the recovery room. Have a seat."

Duh, I'm his daughter, lady, if you bothered to look. Kieran and I sat down in the beige-green waiting room. I picked up a magazine and absently started flipping through it, without even checking to see what I'd grabbed.

"Do you have plans for next year? Have you chosen a university?" Kieran asked. He slid down the chair and crossed his ankles, fingers entwined and his thumbs tapping a pattern against his shirt.

"I do, in a sense. Just not sure where yet. U of T, Queens, a couple of places in the U.S. with good med programs."

His eyebrows popped up. "You want ta be a doctor?"

"I think so. What about you? D'you plan on heading back to Scotland when school's done?"

"No wey I'd go back to Edinburgh. Dad's family's thar and I've no interest in seein' them ever again. I'm not sure wha' I plan to do." His mouth hung slightly open, his tongue running over his teeth. "I like me dad being gone... Elliot Lake's not so bad." He looked right at me, his eyes saying more than his words. *Because of you.*

I knew better than to say my thoughts out loud. *Come with me*, I wanted to say.

My dad strode through the door, his head down as he flipped through a chart in his hands. His face erased all its seriousness when he saw me. "Zoezey!"

Funny how that nickname sounded so different coming from his lips than Kieran's. *Speaking of* – "Dad, this is Kieran."

Kieran stood and held his hand out, which my father shook. *Score one on politeness.* "We met briefly at the mine the night of the storm. It's nice ta meet you, Dr. Taylor."

I wanted to do a tiny glee clap dance. Kieran sounded like the kind of guy my dad would love. The smile on Dad's face proved my thoughts.

"Great of you to come in with Zoe. I'll make this quick." Dad handed the file to his secretary and beckoned us to follow him into one of the patient rooms. "Hope you're not afraid of needles."

The room had a small desk, a sink, and the metal bed with the rollaway-tissue on top. Kieran sat on the rolling stool so I hopped onto the patient bench.

Dad went to his desk, leaned down, and wrote our names down on some labels. "I'll be right back," he said and disappeared out of the room.

Kieran cleared his throat. "Is he always, uh, this easy going?"

I leaned back against the wall, the crinkle of the paper below me firecrackers to my ears. "I think he's just excited he's got fresh blood."

Kieran raised his eyebrows.

"My dad's got this thing about testing markers in blood. His research stuff is about RBCs, WBCs, platelets, and yadda, yadda, yadda." I laughed at the expression on Kieran's face. "Don't be nervous now. He just wants to check our blood for uranium."

"That's it? He's got no clue about your..." He tugged his earlobe.

"Nothing." I glanced at the door. "He's just gonna compare our results. Hopefully yours and mine aren't too different and it'll get us off the hook."

"I'm not sure –" Kieran said and stopped.

Dad strolled back in, two needles and a tray of vials. "This'll be quick." He pointed to my arm and I began rolling up my sleeve.

"How much do ya plan on taking?" Kieran's round eyes followed the tray. "I think I've only got about ten pints."

The prick of the needle entering my skin grated against my ears. The vacuuming suction as my heart sucked blood through my veins was impossible to ignore.

Dad laughed as he filled a third vial from my arm. "I want to check uranium levels and blood count. Zoe had her WBC count up and I want to make sure it's nothing."

"She, uh, looked tired before, maybe it was a bug." Kieran winked at me when my dad turned to finish up. "I think she looks great."

Dad then winked at me, giving my arm a light squeeze. "Maybe it was a bug." He faced Kieran. "Your turn."

Kieran rolled his sleeve and made a fist. The bruises on his forearm had faded, but four light scratch lines trailed down. He was oblivious to the needle breaking his skin. A little part of me had been curious if the needle would've bent instead of going in, he seemed so tough. The power of his blood pushing into the vial sounded like a waterfall to my ears.

"Quick case history," Dad said, switching to an empty vial. "Do you have any family history of disease or disorders? Anything I might need to be aware of."

Kieran shot a nervous look to me, his head giving the slightest of shakes. "I don't think so."

Dad switched and filled the final vial, putting a cotton ball with a piece of tape on top of Kieran's pin prick. He stepped back shaking the vials. "If you think of anything, say for example your grand-dad had cancer, just tell Zoe and she can let me know. Or pop by here on your own if you want." He stuck the labels on Kieran's vials. "Do you have a family doctor?"

"Not yet." Kieran glanced at me.

He's panicking that he might have to say his dad's in Scotland and he's on his own. I mouthed, "It's okay." My dad wouldn't say anything.

"Just come see me," Dad said, oblivious to Kieran's worry. "I'll help you out." He slipped behind the desk and began jotting down dates on the vials. "It's the least I can offer. I really appreciate you coming in."

"No problem, Dr. Taylor." He stood, slipping his coat back on.

"I'm sure I'll see you around, Kieran." Dad gave me a hug and ushered me out the door. "Give your mom a shout to let her know you were here. It'll—"

"I will, Dad." I tapped my back pocket where my phone was. "See you later."

We headed out of the hospital and back into the Bug.

"Crap! I left my coat in the waiting room." Kieran turned back and started jog back to the building. "Meet me by the door?"

I started the Bug and drove to the entrance. He came walking out, coat slung over his arm and a smile on his face. He jumped into the passenger side. "Good to go. By the way, your dad has one weird nurse." He clapped his hands and rubbed them together. "Can we head back 'n start cookin'? I'm starving!"

"Sounds good to me. I'll make the sauce and you can roll the meatballs." Pulling out of the parking lot, I waved my pass in front of the electronic parking camera and pulled onto the main road when the exit bar shifted upwards.

Chapter 10

Kieran sat quietly watching the scenery from the passenger window as I drove back. I racked my brain, trying to think of some witty conversation or interesting topic to start with him. I still hadn't come up with anything when we pulled into his driveway.

"I'm excited for dinner." Kieran unlocked the front door and flipped on some lights.

I followed him in and giggled. "I hope you aren't expecting anything fancy. It's just noodles."

"But it's homemade, not from a can!"

"Yuck!" I leaned against the kitchen counter as Kieran opened the fridge and grabbed the hamburger and two cans of Coke.

"Do you want a Coke?"

I never drank pop but didn't want to admit it. "Sure."

He pulled two glasses out of the cupboard and handed me one, along with a can. "What do you want me to do?"

I flinched as I pulled the tab on the can and it squealed in my ears as it popped open. I poured some pop into my glass, then set it down to let the fizz settle. "Did you get Brent's email today?"

He drummed his fingers against his Coke can. "What did he want?"

"To cancel tomorrow's practice."

"Really? Is he going out?"

"Maybe." It seemed like Kieran was fishing for information. Or knew something and was trying to avoid having to talk about it. I figured it was the latter. "Do you think something's up? Between him and Seth?"

Kieran straightened. "Because of the other day? When Seth opened his mouth and stuck his foot into it?"

I giggled. "Good analogy."

"I think they're fine. Guys don't get into things like girls do."

"Things? You mean like feelings?"

"Something like that."

"Brent's dad probably needs the gym or something."

He nodded absently, probably already losing interest in the conversation.

Brent had only written they couldn't train and then suggested they get together Saturday or Monday. *Let it go. Even Kieran thinks Seth and Brent are fine.* I turned my focus to making dinner. "Do you like vegetables?"

He pretended to look nervous, giving a scared face before exaggerating as he chewed his lower lip. "It depends what you've got inside the brown bag."

I stood in front of the bag to stop him from peeking. "I've got horrid tasting things inside of here. Did I forget to tell you my mother's a witch?"

"Oh no! Does she carry a wand?"

"Nope, just does evil spells with dried out dead animals and icky stuff like that." I giggled, unable to keep a serious face.

"Shoot!" He opened a cupboard beside the stove and began banging stuff around in it.

"What's wrong?"

"I don't have a cauldron." He spun around, hiding something behind his back. "Will a frying pan do?" He held a worn non-stick pan in his right hand.

I burst out laughing. "It'll be perfect."

"I'm not a fan of aubergine."

"Say what?"

He began washing the frying pan and pulled out a pot to fill with water for the noodles. "You asked me about vegetables. I don't really like aubergines."

I pulled onions, mushrooms, and peppers out of bag. "I have no clue what that is."

"That's good. Then you won't have any." He stepped close beside me and peered into the bag. "I only see Bolognese, noodles, and bread. We're safe."

He smelled really good. Musky and some really good cologne or something. My breath caught at his nearness. I pretended to look inside the bag, but stared at his mouth with my peripheral vision. Would he kiss me later? I swallowed. My body had strange feelings when I was near him. Did he have that, too? I blinked and slowly let out the breath I'd been holding. "Aubergine and Bolognese? Are you sure you speak English?"

He smiled. "Bolognese is meat sauce." He snapped his fingers. "Eggplant! That's it. You guys call aubergine eggplant."

I made a face. "Yuck."

He touched the tip of my nose lightly with his finger. "That's my girl."

We stared at each other, neither of us saying anything, but the silence didn't feel awkward. A bubbling sound and metal slightly shaking caught my super sensitive ears. "The water's boiling," I whispered.

"Guess we should start cooking."

I blinked and glanced around me. "Right. Do you want to cut the onions or roll the meatballs?"

He shrugged. "I'll do the meatballs. Sounds like the manly thing to do."

"Sounds good." I pulled a little spice mix out of the bag. "Add this to the hamburger before you start rolling. My mom made this mix up. It's awesome."

Kieran raised a single eyebrow. "Your mom?"

"Stop it. She's not a witch." I swatted his hand playfully. "Get rolling, and maybe turn the water on the stove down before it's all boiled away."

"Yes, ma'am." He saluted and went to work.

I cut the onions and other vegetables then added them to the meatballs when they were cooked. Kieran added more water to the pan, and when it boiled again, he added the noodles. He hopped up and sat on the counter while I added sauce and cut the bread. He pulled a ball out of a drawer and began tossing and catching it as he waited.

He slid off the counter when I checked the noodles. "They're ready." I poured them into the strainer and he set two plates on the counter.

"I'll set the table." Kieran grabbed two new glasses and then put them back in the cupboard. He went to the china cabinet and pulled out two wine glasses.

My hand paused midair with a spoonful of sauce.

He whistled as he strolled by me to the fridge and pulled out a gallon of milk. "Our white wine." He grinned.

"Awesome." I poured the sauce and carried the two plates to the table. Kieran grabbed the platter of bread. He set the table so we sat beside each other at a corner, facing each other.

He sat down and rubbed his hands. "This smells unbelievable!" He held up his wine glass of milk. "Cheers."

I clinked his glass with mine. "Cheers."

Kieran twirled his fork and took a bite. He popped a meatball in his mouth and groaned. "Oh, my freakin' goodness. This is so good!" He took another bite.

It was fun watching him enjoy the meal. Using the last piece of bread to mop up his plate, he grinned. "You'll have to tell your mom the meatball spice is the bomb."

"You can have the little container I brought along. And, there's leftovers."

His eyes lit up. "Seriously? For me?"

I shrugged, loving how he acted like I'd made his day. "I figured you could use it. With your dad gone... it probably sucks."

He picked at the bread crumbs. "He didn't really cook." He met my gaze. "Is it bad that I don't really miss him? I like the quiet."

It was my turn to pick at the paper napkin. "I don't think I blame you. I mean, I don't really know your dad. I've only met him once." What should I say? He seemed like a jerk and a bad guy who beat his son? "You seem... more relaxed."

"That happens when you get to sleep through the night."

"I get that. Never knew sleep was so important." I coughed, realizing I had just steered the conversation away from him and toward me. "In a different way, of course."

"It helps."

I felt like a jerk. He was trying to talk and it sounded like I was trying to steal the show. I felt like Rylee. "Sorry."

"Why?" He put his hand on my knee. "You want to know something? I'm starting to feel happy. For the first time in forever."

The warmth of his skin made its way through my jeans. It seemed to spread up my leg to my inner thigh. I ran my tongue over my lips. "I'm glad. But Kieran, what are you going to do if he doesn't come back?"

"What?" He blinked.

"How are you going to pay the bills? Or take care of the house? You're seventeen."

"Oh, the bills." He scratched behind his ear. "There's money. He sends it. I'll be fine."

"I don't think it's that easy."

"I'll figure it out as I go."

"It takes a lot of money to run a house, pay taxes, do all that stuff. I wouldn't even know where to start."

Kieran eyes grew big. "I-I have no idea either." He shook his head and then shrugged. "My dad said he'd take care of it from

Scotland." He grinned. "No worries." He began clearing the dishes.

I sat a moment before jumping up to help. His heart rate had sped up and again I wished I'd kept my mouth shut. He was probably in a panic, worrying about whether his dad would actually take care of things.

"Do you want to wash or dry?"

I smiled. His heart rate had settled down to a regular rhythm, showing me he'd relaxed. "How about I wash? Then you can put the stuff away where it goes as you dry?"

"Perfect."

We worked a few minutes without talking. "What do you think of school compared to back in Scotland?"

"It's different. Some of it is harder, some is easier. Math is easy. We're doing what I learned last year. I don't get history class. North American history is not something we studied in detail." He paused, but I could hear his hesitation loud and clear so I waited. "I like art."

I handed him a dinner plate. "I suck at art. Me and drawing don't see eye to eye."

He tilted his head and watched me. "I had the feeling you didn't suck at anything."

Heat flushed my cheeks. The compliment made me giggle. "I can't draw. Even my stickmen are barely recognizable."

"I like drawing." He said it so quietly, no normal person would have heard it.

I had the feeling drawing, painting, or anything along those lines didn't measure up in his dad's eyes. Something my mom always said to me as a kid popped into my head. "Can you make me something and sign it? One day it might be worth millions." Mom usually added millions of kisses, but when you're five years old that sounded priceless. Saying it to Kieran would – just not be right.

He smiled. "Sure. I'll have to think of something you'd like."

"Anything." *As long as it's done by you.*

His smile widened. "No, you deserve something that's totally yours."

I pulled the plug on the drain, paranoid he might see the excitement on my face.

A pulsation echoed against my ears. "Your phone's about to—"

Kieran's cell phone, lying on the kitchen table, began ringing. He walked over and picked it up. "Hullo?"

I heard Rylee's voice clearly through the line. "Hi, Kieran. I hope I'm not bothering you."

"It's fine."

"Cool. I'm just sitting in my bedroom..." I tried not to roll my eyes at Rylee's dramatic pause. "I'm doing homework. I don't get what we did in math today. Could you help me?"

"I don't have me stuff here. I can try an' help over the phone."

I dried my hands and put the Tupperware container I'd filled earlier into the fridge. It was next to impossible to avoid hearing Rylee's voice. She did struggle in math but, seriously, did she have to call Kieran now? It wasn't like she knew I was over here. I hadn't said anything and she wasn't trying to make this into a competition. I sighed and walked around into the living room to put my coat on.

"Rylee," Kieran said from the kitchen, "can you hold on a moment?" He leaned against the doorframe between the two rooms. "Zoe, are you leaving?"

I zipped my coat up and smiled, determined not to show my annoyance at Rylee. "I have homework to do too."

"You could do it here."

Now that I'd put my jacket on, it didn't seem right to change my mind. It would be totally obvious I'd tried to run because of Rylee. "I left my bag at home."

"Do you want to go get it and come back?"

Tempting... except, "My mom won't go for it. If she knew I came here and your dad's out of the country, she'll ground me till I'm thirty."

He stared intently at me. Those beautiful eyes could be my undoing. He swallowed hard and then whispered, barely audible, knowing I'd pick it up no problem. "Let me get rid of Rylee. Give me a sec."

I nodded and slipped back into the kitchen while he dropped onto the living room couch. I needed to grab the few things to take back home.

He was talking about going over one of the algebra problems and breaking it down to the basics.

I slipped down the hall to the bathroom. Just by the door, I paused to take my coat off. I looked at Kieran's room. The lock on his door had been unscrewed. He'd even fixed and painted so you couldn't tell it had even been there. Thank goodness.

When I came back to the living room, he had his jacket on and runners. "I put your groceries on your passenger seat and started your car. Hope you don't mind. It's getting cold out." He grinned sheepishly.

"How was Rylee?" I asked as I put my shoes back on.

"Fine. Flirty. The usual." He checked his watch. "She's not getting math from today. At all."

"Is she coming over now?" The words were out of my mouth before I could stop them.

"Rylee?" He stared at me again with those eyes that seemed to be able to read more into me than I wanted to share. "Would you stay if I said she was coming?"

I shook my head, afraid to speak.

"She's not coming. I didn't invite her."

Was he trying to say something more? Like he had invited me but not her? If I had the courage I'd ask, but when it came to Kieran I seemed to only have insecurities.

"I can walk you to your car if you'd like." He stood by the door, his hand on the doorknob.

"Sure." My hands went instantly sweaty and I licked my lips. The moment suddenly seemed a build up to a kiss. Half of me couldn't wait, the other half wanted to run and hide from the nervousness. I shoved my hands into my coat pockets and walked toward the door.

Kieran held it open for me and followed close behind. He slipped beside me on the path from the porch to the driveway. "Thanks again for dinner."

We reached the Bug. "You're welcome."

"I can make you dinner sometime. Something Scottish... if you want."

"I'd like that." I turned and leaned against the car. The coldness of the metal seeped through my jeans and against my skin. I shivered.

Kieran stepped closer, his shoes brushing against mine.

We both looked down at the same time and our foreheads touched. I shivered again, but not from the cold.

"Zoezey?" he whispered.

I slowly brought my head up and my nose brushed lightly against his. My eyes closed instinctly but not before I saw Kieran do the same. His lips pressed against mine a moment before he moved them back slightly. Cool air blew across the warm wetness his lips had left on mine. I moved my mouth to cover the small distance he had created and kissed him with an urgency I didn't know I had.

Kieran's fingers found their way to my chin and cheeks. One hand moved to bury itself into my hair and the other stroked my cheek before trailing down and tugging lightly on my collar to pull me closer. My hands found their way inside his jacket and around his waist. I'd never felt muscles that tight or delicious. *How would it feel to run my fingers against his skin?* I moaned, thinking back to his near naked body earlier today. I had no idea what to do and letting Kieran take the lead seemed the natural thing to do. I just went with the flow.

He opened his mouth a little wider and gently pressed his tongue against mine. Kieran lightly touched the tip of my tongue and a new kind of excitement exploded inside my head and throughout my body. His tongue disappeared into his mouth as he kissed me again. A moment later his tongue slipped back into my mouth. It felt like the most intimate moment I had ever experienced. I moved my head slightly to catch my breath.

Kieran did the same and then smiled as his eyes met mine. "I'll see you tomorrow at school." He slowly stepped back, his hands finding mine and curling over them. "Text me when you get home?"

I nodded, not trusting my voice.

He let go of my hands and opened the car door for me. I settled in and he leaned in, stealing on quick kiss on my lips before closing the door. He jogged back to the house as I put the Bug into reverse and pulled out on to the road.

Driving home, I kept replaying the image and feeling of his lips against mine. I'm no expert on kissing, but that was a great kiss. There had definitely been magic in the moment we had just shared.

Chapter 11

Brent

As I slammed the car door shut my stomach growled, reminding me I hadn't eaten since lunch. Usually after last class I scarfed down a sandwich or burger or something to get me through till after training. Since we weren't meeting up in the gym today, I hadn't bothered to grab anything. I was hungry now.

Actually, I was pretty much starving all the time. Probably from training, and the fact I'd put on muscle. I wasn't muscle-man like Seth, but I definitely had some strength building starting to happen. I jogged up the steps and around the porch to the front door.

It annoyed me that I even wanted to compare myself to Seth. Whatever his problem was – it was his – not mine. None of us got to choose which sense became heightened, just like I didn't have a choice on who my parents were, or that my family had money. After his stupid outburst earlier this week, he acted like nothing had happened the next day at school so I let it go. If he wanted to be an ass again, I wouldn't let it slide.

"Hello?" I called out. Dad's car was parked in his usual spot but Mom's was out. The alarm system beeped to let me know it hadn't been turned off. No one was in the house. *Weird.* I hit the code to turn the alarm off and headed to the kitchen.

Making three sandwiches, I skimmed through the newspaper as I ate them. I never read the paper but thought there might be something about the John Doe. It seemed crazy they hadn't found anything yet, but there was no mention in the paper about him. Only interesting article was about a string of break-ins the police were starting to think were related. And it was still boring.

I grabbed a Gatorade from the fridge and reread the article. One policeman was quoted that he thought there were more related robberies, but people were either too stupid to notice things were missing, or they were the kind of people who couldn't claim the things were gone.

What a dickhead cop. I tossed the paper in the recycle bin and brought my plate to the sink.

The house seemed oddly quiet without anyone in it. I checked the grandfather clock in the hallway. Half past five and no one home but me? I grabbed my phone and dialed Mom's cell.

She picked it up on the fourth ring. "Hello, Sweetie."

"Hey, Mom. Sorry to bug you, I was just wondering where you were."

"I'm on my way home. I had a hair appointment and just grabbed some Thai food for dinner."

"Is Dad with you?"

"No." She paused. "Why do you ask?"

"His car's in the driveway but he's not here."

"He should be home. He called a few hours ago to say he had stuff to do at the house. Maybe he's in the garage."

"I don't think so. The house alarm was on when I got back." Dad was no mechanic. The only stuff in the garage was the lawn equipment the maintenance guys used.

"He probably had a meeting and had one of the office drivers pick him up."

"Yeah." She was probably right. He wouldn't be in the gym. He never went there unless he wanted to have a meeting. "Thai sounds good. I'll see you in a bit."

"Bye, Sweetie."

After I stuffed my cell back into my jeans pocket, I tied my shoes back up. I figured I'd go and check the gym. Stepping outside, I ran back in to grab my coat. The temperature had dropped drastically in the past hour. Winter was coming and I had the feeling it was going to be a cold one this year.

Zipping up my jacket I jogged around the house and down the lane to the gymnasium behind. Maybe I'd do some stuff on the equipment before Mom got back. I had workout stuff in the locker room. A little extra wouldn't hurt.

I slowed to a walk when I reached the sidewalk and tried the door. It was open and oddly, the alarm wasn't on when I stepped inside. I remembered setting it last night before leaving. "Dad?" I called out down the hall.

No response.

I shrugged and headed into the gym, flipping the lights on. The hum as they warmed reminded me of Zoe and I wondered what she was up to this evening. I pulled my phone out as I headed to the lockers to change. Hopefully she wasn't hanging out with Kieran. Three years in high school and when I finally realize I like her, a new guy shows up to steal her away? I had no problem with Kieran, it just sucked he happened to like the same girl I did.

I started to text but stopped and hit her number to call her instead.

She picked up after the third ring. "Hey, Brent!"

I grinned. She sounded excited. "Hi!"

"You at the gym?"

"Yeah." I scratched my head. "How'd you know?"

She laughed. A sexy, husky sounding laugh. How had I never noticed how cool it sounded before? "I can hear the echo against the walls as you talk and... the lights warming up inside the gym."

I held my breath, wondering if she could hear anything else.

"Who's with you?"

"No one. I'm on my own."

She said nothing for a moment. "Are you sure? Forget it. It's probably your heartbeat echoing against the walls. It just sounded like I heard two."

"It's just me." I swallowed, then added quietly. "Unless you want to join me." Would she get what I meant? I stopped walking and leaned my hand against the wall, shaking my head. I'd probably just screw up our friendship.

My fingers reacted against the brick and the room behind it came into view. "Holy sh—" I nearly dropped the phone. "Zoe, I gotta go."

"Wait! What's going on? Why's your heart racing? I can hear it. What happened that's got you so scared? I'm coming over."

"No! Don't!" I dropped my voice barely above a whisper knowing she'd hear it no problem. I inched my way to the door. My hand shook as I pressed it against the wood of the door of the conference room. Someone was in there, bent over by the desk. "Zoe. Someone's here. I don't know if they're trying to rob the place or what's going on. Call the cops. Don't come here on your own. I need to check the room again. The room's turned upside down and someone's in there. I don't think they know I'm here."

"Don't hang up," she begged. "I'll call the police on our home phone."

I closed my eyes and held my breath as I focussed on the room. Whoever was in there had torn the room apart. I focussed on the desk and, even with my eyes closed, squinted trying to see the person better. A guy. I couldn't see his head but he hadn't moved. Then I saw the briefcase flung open on the table.

My dad's.

I dropped my phone and threw my shoulder into the door. It was unlocked and swung open hard – so fast I nearly fell from the momentum. I ran around the desk shouting, "Dad! Dad!"

Zoe had said she heard two heartbeats.

He had to be alive.

His suit was crumpled, his nose bloody, and blood also oozed from a cut by his temple. I place my index and middle finger on his neck like they did in the movies. He had a pulse. Thank goodness.

He flinched against my hand and moaned.

I dropped down so my head was at the same level as his. "Dad! What happened?"

His eyes fluttered and closed. He groaned and moved so he lay on his back on top of the desk. "Brent?" His voice croaked. He grimaced as he tried to swallow. "I'm okay." His hand came up and he grabbed at the air, trying to find me.

I held my hand out and his gripped my wrist.

He pulled himself to a sitting position and looked around the room. "Insolent bastard!"

"Who?"

Dad pounded the desk with his fist. "I don't know. What a mess!" He picked his briefcase up. "Bastard stole my money!"

"Who?" I repeated. I lowered my voice. "They could still be here." I glanced around the room, ready to go out in the hall and check every room with my ability. "Who did this?"

"I have no clue." He pinched his nose and swore. "I came in here to use the safe and found the room like this. Some guy must have been hiding behind the door and hit me from behind. I never saw who it was." He flicked is wrist, trying to shake the blood off his hand. "Son of a bitch!" He grabbed his ribs and seemed to be trying hold or apply pressure against them.

"Are you okay?" I kept my arms at my sides, not comfortable touching him now that I knew he was alive and all right.

"I'm fine." With his free arm, he reached for his phone he always kept in the inside pocket of his suit jacket. He came out empty-handed. "He stole my bloody phone!"

"I've got mine." I reached for it and then remembered I'd dropped it by the door. I went to get it and could hear Zoe's voice calling from it.

"Brent! Brent! Can you hear me? Brent!"

I picked it up. "I'm here. I'm okay. My dad's hurt, but I think he's okay."

"I heard. Do you need me to call the police?"

"No. My dad's going to. He needs my phone."

She paused. "You sure you're all right?"

I smiled at the concern in her voice. "Yeah. I'll call you later, 'kay?"

"I'll be waiting."

My dad cautiously bent over and grabbed his briefcase. He started gathering papers off the desk and couple off the floor before giving up.

"I'll get that." I walked over and set the phone on the desk before reaching for the loose sheets on the ground.

Dad picked up an overturned chair and set it upright. He sat down gingerly, his eyebrows mashed together as he glared at the room.

"Do you want to call the cops?" I stacked the papers in a pile and set them on top of his briefcase.

He waved his hand. "No. I'll take care of this myself. Police aren't going to be able to do anything. I'll also have to get someone in here tomorrow to clean the place up." He pulled his jacket off and wiped his nose with his sleeve. "Dammit!"

I stood there, unsure of what to say.

Dad sighed. "Well, they got what they came for."

"How do you know?" What was going on?

"I had ten thousand dollars cash in my briefcase."

Seriously? Who carried that kind of money? And in cash? I squinted, trying to see if he'd banged his head too hard. Something wasn't adding up, but I had no intention of asking him about it.

He grimaced as he stood. He slowly headed toward the door. "I'm going to shower and clean up."

"Shouldn't I take you to the hospital first?"

"I'm not going to the hospital."

Why did I have to have the most stubborn father in the world? "Maybe you bruised a rib." The words sounded lame, even to me.

"I'll be fine. If I go to the hospital, then they'll call the cops."

"Which is what we should be doing right now. Ten thousand dollars is a lot of money."

He closed his eyes and took a breath and exhaled it. "Brent, just leave it alone. It was more like a couple thousand. I was just exaggerating."

I shrugged. He was hiding something and had no intention of saying any more. Maybe he knew who had done this? I swallowed. Or could he be trying to protect me? The argument with Seth echoed inside my head. Nahhh, Seth wouldn't... would he? We'd all changed since the storm, I just wondered how much.

My silence let Dad think I agreed with him. "Good."

I walked toward where he stood by the door. "I'm going to check the rest of the place. Make sure no one's here."

"They got what they came for."

What if whoever it was came back? "Did the guy have a weapon? What if he's in the house? Mom's going to be home any moment!"

"The alarm's on. Nobody can get in."

"It's off. I went inside when I got home from school."

"Why didn't you put it on when you left the house?"

"'Cause I was walking over here!"

Dad blew a breath out. "When you walked here, did you see anyone?"

I shook my head.

"They're gone." He seemed quite sure of himself. "I'm going to shower." He walked out of the room.

"I'm still checking the house." Dad had no idea what I could do with my hands. It wouldn't take long. If someone was there, I'd call the cops.

"Whatever," he called from the hallway.

I glanced around the room. It looked like a tornado had hit the place. I knew by tomorrow after school there would be no sign of the struggle. No one would ever know. Well, I would and Zoe would kind of know as well. I planned on telling the others and looking Seth straight in the eye as I did.

"Brent!" Dad hollered from the hallway. "What the hell have you done to my gym?"

I rolled my eyes. *Here we go.*

Chapter 12

I ignored Dad's annoyed call from the gym and slipped out to check the house. It took me barely any time to check the large house. As I walked down the winding staircase, I wished I'd timed it. I'd make an awesome detective with this skill. Mom came in so I helped her carry dinner and groceries into the kitchen. Dad came in shortly after. He had cleaned up, and when Mom saw the shiner starting to show, he brushed it off blaming it on a wild ball from playing racquetball after work. He told the story so well, I almost believed him.

I excused myself after dinner, lying that I had a lot of homework. I stayed up in my room and chilled.

All night my thoughts kept coming back to Seth and how he could have easily gotten into the gym, turned the alarm off, or just waited till my dad was there and snuck in. The guy probably had the ability to taste money now, and got greedy – then went a step too far.

In between the bouts of frustration and anger, I thought about Zoe. I was kidding myself if I believed I really stood a chance. I'd waiting too long before making my move. Now Kieran liked her and the feeling seemed mutual. It didn't take a rocket scientist to figure that one out. Well, except for Rylee. She still hadn't clued in.

The next morning, after a long night of little sleep, I sent the gang a message: **Meet me at PHP after school at 4:00pm.**

I decided to skip school, faking a bad headache to Mom, and couldn't help but be relieved when Dad told her to let me sleep in.

He never agreed to missing class, so she didn't argue. I went back to my bedroom and worked on fine tuning my touch-seeing sense.

Mom brought me a bowl of homemade soup for lunch and a nasty looking vegetable shake. "It'll help flush the bad toxins out of your body and get rid of your headache. It's better than any aspirin or ibuprofen."

"I'm not drinking that."

She crossed her arms and stared down at me sitting on my bed. I felt six years old suddenly. "I am not leaving until you drink the entire glass. If you think it tastes bad now, wait till you try drinking it warm."

I sipped and gagged. "I can't drink this!"

She laughed. "Don't be such a wimp."

Seriously? My mom just called me a wimp? I gulped it down and shuddered. Twice. I wiped my mouth with the back of my hand and gave her the glass.

"That's a good boy." She kissed my forehead. "Now eat your soup and try to get some rest."

My throat reflex had a mind of its own. I swallowed hard and mentally told my stomach to cool. "Thanks, Mom."

She left the room and I sighed. The awful taste in my mouth needed to be eliminated so I went straight for the chicken noodle soup. It killed the thick taste of spinach and every other dark and disgusting garden vegetable mixed in. Mom made the best soup. I enjoyed every bite and set the empty bowl on my desk.

My phone's red light flashed from its location charging on my desk.

Zoe had messaged: **Everything all right?**

I replied: **I'm good. Just chilling. Taking a personal day. I'll see you at PHP after school?**

I crawled back to bed. The headache I faked ended up as bad karma and showed up. I wanted to blame it on the horrible drink, but crawling under the covers and hiding in the dark seemed all the

RADIUM HALOS - PART 2

thought process my brain could handle. Images flashed through my head when I shut my eyes tight. I clenched my hands and toes as the agony turned into a migraine.

I don't know when, but I managed to fall asleep or pass out into oblivion.

An annoying *beep-beep-beep* sound woke me. Some truck must be backing up. Probably a dump truck or cleaning vehicle for dad's conference office. I bolted upright and checked my clock radio for the time. Almost three. School would be out in ten minutes.

I sat up and swung my legs over the side of the bed. My migraine had disappeared. I felt good – fantastic, actually. Maybe the migraine had shown up from the toxins in my system spilling into my blood or brain or some kind of scientific explanation Heidi would know. Mom's disgusting veggie drink actually cleaned my system. Whatever. I felt better.

I hopped off the bed and dropped to do a set of push-ups. As I pumped my arms up and down, I looked through the floor with my hands. I blinked in surprise. The room below was dark but I could see clearer than normal, almost like a pair of night vision goggles – but not that good. I'd have to ask Mom to make me the veggie drink again.

My watched beeped, reminding me of the time. I needed to shower and jet. Fifteen minutes later I jogged down the stairs and grabbed a banana from the kitchen. Mom was reading by the window.

"Feeling better?" she asked.

"Loads. I might even ask you to make me that drink again."

She laughed. "I will. Be good to have one before bed tonight. You'll sleep like a baby tonight and back to normal tomorrow."

I nearly choked on my banana. She knew nothing of what normal was for me anymore. "I'm heading down to PHP to meet the gang."

"Don't eat anything greasy."

"Pardon?"

"Stay away from French fries or their onion rings. The grease will clog your system and ruin everything the drink just cleared."

I saluted. "Yes, ma'am."

She grabbed a napkin, balled it up, and threw it at me. "Get going, silly. I'm glad you feel better."

I walked around the counter and hugged her. "Love you, Mom."

"Love you, too, Sweetie."

The drive to PHP took another ten minutes. Kieran's bike and Seth's truck were already there, but I didn't see the Bug. I pressed my hand against the building and pretended to fix my shoe as a couple walked by. Heidi, Rylee, Seth, and Kieran were all sitting in our usual spot.

I went in to meet them. "Where's Zoe?"

Rylee, sitting close to Kieran, looked up. "Hi to you, too. She said she had to go home to change. She'll be here in a moment. So, I ordered our outfits."

Seth sat beside Heidi wearing a leather jacket I'd never seen before. I glanced down his arm and noticed new watch. Something big and expensive.

What the hell? I unfortunately ignored Rylee's chatter and cut her off. "Been shopping, Seth?"

He grinned and pulled the sleeve up on his jacket, showing off the watch.

Seriously? The guy robbed and beat up my father, and now had the balls to show it off? Screw him!

Rylee, the queen of fashion, leaned forward. "Wow, that's very nice."

"Thanks. I just got it." Seth shoved his arm closer to Rylee's face.

"I thought you were broke." I couldn't believe it. The guy had the balls to show it off in front of me. Some friend. We'd been buds since kindergarten. Scratch that. I hated him now. I clenched my fists, trying to keep things in check in front of everyone. This was not the place to break his jaw.

"I am." Seth shot me a weird look. "My dad found an awesome deal and decided to get me it as an early grad gift."

I grabbed a chair from the table beside and flipped it around so I sat on it backwards. I rested my arms on the back and leaned forward, faking interest. "Why didn't he save it for grad then?"

"I don't know. Maybe it was an early birthday present." He shrugged. "I wasn't paying attention to the whys."

I pulled my phone out. "Why don't I give him a shout and ask him? I wouldn't mind one myself."

"Wha'?" He pulled his coat over the watch. "No! Don't call him."

Heidi glanced at me, then Seth, and then back at me. "What's going on?"

"Ohhh..." Rylee glared at Seth. "It's you." She pointed an accusing finger at him.

Seth pushed her hand away. "I don't know what you're talking about."

Kieran and I looked at each other. I had a feeling he knew what Seth had done.

Rylee crossed her arms. She hissed at him, "You're not the only one who watches the news or reads the paper! You bastard! How did you think we wouldn't figure it out? It's been you robbing those shops and stealing stuff."

Seth straightened. "What the hell?"

Chapter 13

Zoe

"Zoe, I'd like to talk to you a moment." Dad stood in Mom's kitchen, his doctor's face on.

"Can it wait? I'm supposed to be at PHP with the gang." I checked my watch. They'd already be there. I tilted my head and listened to Dad's body. His heart rate was elevated and his breathing was off. "Where's Mom?" Panic inched into my veins.

"She's at work."

I puffed out a breath. "Does she know you're here?"

He shook his head. "I didn't want to get her worried." He rubbed his eye. "I ran a million tests on your blood work. Yours and Kieran's."

The anxiety wanted to return but I forced it to stay dormant. I leaned against the counter, trying to look casual but needing it for support. "A million? Sounds like you're trying to find a needle in a haystack."

"No. It's the opposite actually." He set the folder he was holding onto the counter and spread the pages out. "These are yours." He pointed to graphs and charts and all these other medical things and then pointed to three other pages. "Those are Kieran's."

Everything sort of pointed to what the gang and I already knew; Kieran didn't have a super-sense. I played dumb. "What's the big deal?"

"Some of your readings are off the charts." He leaned in and I could clearly hear the excitement in his voice. "I was originally so worried about the possibility of radiation in your system. Neither you nor Kieran have any. Remember I took your blood right after the night in the mine?" He didn't wait for me to answer. "There was radium in your system. Trace amounts, possibly, but my notes showed a lot more. I don't know what happened, but your bodies turned it into something else. DNA binding agents have morphed the radiation." He pulled a coloured printed page of some kind of strand of puzzle. "This is your DNA from the other day."

I started at him, not getting what he was trying to show me. "What am I looking at?"

"Right there, see?" He tapped several places in the strand.

I squinted and tried to see something out of the ordinary. "Dad, I have no clue what I'm looking for. Am I supposed to find something that doesn't follow a pattern?"

He grinned and pulled a pencil out of his pocket. "Look right there." He circled something. "What do you see?"

I picked up the page and stared. "Some kind of fuzzy circle or ring?"

"It's a halo."

My eyebrows shot up. "Like something an angel has?"

He laughed. "Not quite. It's more like a nimbus or aurora. It's surrounded itself around a molecule of radium which attached to your DNA."

"Say what?"

"I'm calling it a radium halo. You've got these radium halos everywhere." He began pacing. "These halos surrounded the radium in your body and protected you. It's scientifically impossible, but with the things I've been experimenting with, I'm starting to question the impossible."

Should I tell him about my sonar hearing? I swallowed, not sure what to do. "If there's radiation in my body, shouldn't I be sick? Or dying?" It seemed surreal to even say it out loud.

"Yes!" he shouted.

"Uh, I don't think you should sound so excited." I knew I wasn't sick, the whole gang knew.

"Sorry. I didn't mean it like that. It's just... it's just... mind-blowing! You aren't sick. Your blood work," he grabbed another sheet from the pile, "is perfectly normal. Better than normal. No red flags for danger."

"That's cool."

He glanced over the charts. "This is between you and me." He met my gaze, his face serious.

I suddenly had the feeling he wasn't looking at me like his little girl, but as someone older.

"I haven't told anyone. Not your mom or any of the doctors I work with. I have an intern who actually found the marker. He has no idea whose DNA or blood work he's working on." Dad pointed to the halo again. "This is just between you and me. Till we can figure it out." He stared intently at me. "Have you noticed any particular changes since the storm?"

Here was my chance. I could say something and maybe regret it or regret not saying anything. "A few things seem different."

He leaned forward. "Like what?"

Where to start or how much did I tell him? I decided baby steps would be the best way to start. "My balance seems easier."

He nodded. "Yes and you've leaned out. Your mother called me, worried about your weight, but I wasn't too worried."

"I've been working out at Brent's gym."

"All of you? The usual crew: Brent, Seth, Rylee, and Heidi?"

"Yeah."

"Do you think they'd let me do some blood work?"

His excitement and need to push the barriers was getting lame. He wasn't interested in me, he was interested in the halos. "I have no idea, Dad."

"I'm just wondering if any of them have the same results as yours."

The image of me inside a cage like a lab rat popped into my head. I was joined by more little rats with my friend's faces. "You said Kieran had no markers. Maybe something weird is just going on with me."

He pursed his lips. "Maybe. But I'd need to compare their DNA and blood work."

I checked my watch again. The gang needed to hear what Dad had figured out. Maybe if we told him, he could find a cure. I didn't know what to say or even think. "If you let me get going, I'll ask them while we're at PHP."

"Are you bribing your father?" A single eyebrow rose above his eye, the other one crushed slightly down.

I grinned. "Maybe a little."

"Go then. But promise me you'll ask."

"Maybe. If you promise not to nag." I left him in the kitchen and headed down the hall to the front door.

"Zoezey?"

"Yeah, Dad?" I called back, tying up my shoe.

He came running around the corner, his eyes wide and his mouth in a big "O". "I knew it!" He snapped his finger. "It's just a hunch, but to actually make the discovery..." He shook his head.

My stomach dropped. "What are you talking about?"

"Nothing." He waved his hand. "I just thought of something, but I need to try a few equations and see if the numbers add up."

"Huh?" The odd beating of his heart put me on guard.

"It's nothing. I-I'm jumping ahead of myself. Go see your friends and enjoy your Friday night." He turned and headed back down the hall to the kitchen.

I listened to him stack and straighten his papers. It wouldn't be long before science proved what was going on with my body. Thank goodness Brent had asked us all to get together. We really needed to talk.

Chapter 14

I stood outside PHP locking the Bug. I froze when I heard Seth and Brent from inside.

"What the hell?"

"You stole from other people too? I thought nailing my dad was low, but ten thousand wasn't enough?"

The anger and disbelief in Brent's voice sent me racing into the building.

"Wait!" I called as I ran to my friends. I grabbed Brent's arm. Kieran jumped up and held on to me.

Seth climbed on the bench and hopped over the small wooden wall that separated the booth from the aisle behind. "I don't know what you guys are talking about." He moved out of hitting reach and stared at Brent.

Kieran hugged me but I refused to let go of Brent until I heard his heart rate slow and his fist finally relax.

Heidi slipped out of the booth and walked around the booths to stand by Seth.

Rylee stared at Kieran holding me. "You *are* with her? How could you be interested in her over me?"

Brent pulled his arm, and me along with it, toward him. I crashed into him and wrapped his arm around my waist to keep me from falling.

Kieran turned to Rylee. "Not everyone and everything in this town is about you!"

Seth leaned over the little booth wall. "Yeah, Rylee."

"Shut up!" Brent and I yelled at the same time.

"Guys," Heidi whispered. "Can we please take this outside? Everyone's looking."

I stepped back from Brent and heard his voice, way below a whisper, "Zoe... I... Why not –"

Rylee spoke, cutting off the rest of Brent's sentence. "Let's go."

We followed Rylee single file out of PHP. Kieran threw two twenty dollar bills on the table to cover what nobody had touched. I made a mental note to make sure we all paid him back later.

The air had chilled considerably and snowflakes floated down. The grey skies seemed to hint that there would be more.

"So what the hell is going on?" Seth leaned against the Bug, oblivious of the snow.

Brent scoffed. "Don't act like you don't know."

"I heard Brent find his dad last night." I didn't understand how Seth could have done this to his best friend. "Why would you hurt him?"

"Hurt who? Brent's dad?" Seth crossed his arms over his chest. "I didn't touch Brent's dad."

Rylee snorted. "Just like you didn't rob any of those other stores."

Seth shook his head and swallowed. He grimaced like the taste in his mouth made him sick. "I haven't stolen anything." He inhaled. "I smell a rat." He exhaled. "Fine. My dad bought the watch and hid it. I found it along with the grad card. I just put it on to try it out. He's working today so I figured nobody would figure it out. I'll put it back as soon as I get home." He waved his hands. "That's my crime. I have *not* robbed any stores or touched your freakin' father, Brent!"

What was happening to our group? We'd always been best friends. It seemed like everything was crashing down and ending.

Heidi stepped into the middle of our circle. Her little feet made a flower path in the building snow on the ground. "We need to slow down. I don't know what's going on but, come on, Seth didn't rob those places in the news. He's like a bull in a china shop." She turned and touched Brent's arm. "I don't know what happened to your dad, but is he okay?"

Brent nodded. "He's okay. Except he wasn't too impressed with what we've done to the gym. Looks like we're going to need another place to train for a bit." He glanced at Seth. "Sorry for assuming..."

"Me, too," Seth said. "I shouldn't have worn the watch. I just hate how money's so easy for you." He shrugged. "Guess I wanted to show off a bit."

Kieran stood silent beside me, holding my hand. "Maybe we need a night off from each other. Catch our breath."

Heidi nodded. "That's what I was going to suggest. We have to work together, and in order to do that, we need to trust each other."

I thought of the conversation with my dad. "I got here late because my dad and I were talking. He took mine and Kieran's blood the other day. Apparently there are markers in our blood. Some kind of rings binding to our blood cells. My dad saw them."

"In Kieran too?" Rylee asked.

"No, just me. Kieran's showed nothing. However, I think we all have these radium halos. If we're all going to chill tonight..." I swallowed, not sure if they would agree. "Do you think we should tell my dad about our super-senses? I think he's going to figure it out eventually."

"No way!" Rylee shook her head. "He's a flippin' doctor. Next thing you know he's going to be dissecting us. I say we don't tell anyone. It's too dangerous."

I was beginning to think keeping it a secret would end up too costly. "Just think about it. Maybe if we get together tomorrow or Sunday or Monday at school, we could see what each of us thinks?"

Kieran squeezed my hand. "I agree with Zoe."

Rylee rolled her eyes. "Of course you do."

"So do I," said Brent.

"Next time we get together let's just talk about it." I hated the pleading sound in my voice.

"Fine," Ryle said. "I'm going home now. My feet are freezing." She pulled her keys out of her purse. "Seth and Heidi, if you want a ride, I'm leaving now."

Heidi hugged me. "I'd better get going. I'll text you tonight?" She hugged me and whispered in my ear.

"Sounds good." I pulled my hand out of Kieran's and hugged her back. "Bye, Rylee," I called over my shoulder.

Brent coughed, clearing his throat. "You want a ride, Seth? Kieran?"

"Sure, beats riding home with crazy pants." He nodded at Rylee.

"Kieran, you need a ride, too?" Brent didn't sound like he actually meant the offer.

"I'm good. I've got me bike here."

I looked through the parking lot, not seeing the bike. "Is it okay to drive in the snow with it?"

He kissed my forehead. "I'll be fine. Call me later tonight. Maybe we can hang out tomorrow. Just you and me."

"Sounds good." I watched him walk around the corner and wave to Rylee and Heidi as he pulled onto the road. I waved to Seth and Brent also and I hopped into the Bug.

I didn't like the feeling in the pit of my stomach. It seemed to be trying to tell me something.

Whatever it was, I sincerely hoped our friendships could handle it.

Chapter 15

I needed to clear my head and get the ringing in my ears to die down. Nothing seemed to be helping tonight. I kept running over everything that had happened since the night in the mine. My chest grew tight and the walls of my room felt as if they were closing in. I grabbed my winter jacket and tiptoed past dad's office door. The clicking noises confirmed he sat typing on his computer.

I quietly opened the front door and snuck through. It wasn't late and I had nothing to hide, but I wanted to be on my own. Hugging myself against the cold, I stared out into the front yard. The steady falling snow swirled and landed on the recently shovelled walkway and drive. I inhaled deeply, and then slowly released it. A glistening snowflake melted; no match against my warm breath.

Wish I could do the same to the ice growing around the gang.

It had been a crazy afternoon. We were struggling to find answers and were now starting to accuse each other. I pressed my fists tight under my armpits. Could Seth really be involved? It seemed hard to believe.

And what was with Brent today? He seemed... off. Like he was nervous or something. I planned on asking him tomorrow.

A vibration inside the back pocket of my jeans diverted my train of thought. I pulled my phone out and checked the screen. Rylee. "Funny," I mumbled. "She never calls, always texts." I pressed the talk button. "Hey. What's up?"

Silence.

A weird, eerie silence you see in the movies before something bad happened. "Grow up," I mumbled to myself. "Rylee?"

A shuffling sound had me pulling the phone away from ear. "Zoe? Thank goodness! I wasn't sure if you'd pick up. I just snuck out of my house. My mom's gonna kill me if she finds out." She panted, clearly she'd been running. "I think I've figured something out. It's big."

Total movie suspense.

"It's about the murder." She huffed. "About us."

"What are you talking about?"

"I... I don't think I should tell you over the phone." She began whispering, "Someone might hear me. I want to make sure my hunch is right."

"What's going on? Where are you?" I started to panic at the worry in her voice and my moron thinking. "Don't be doing anything dangerous on your own, Rylee."

"Shhh!" Her breath caught. "I think someone's following me."

I heard her heart rate pick up. "Where are you? I'm coming right now in the Bug."

There was a long pause and then she started laughing. "It's a bloody cat. I'm being stalked by a cat." She stopped laughing. "Sorry. I'm just getting paranoid."

I moved back into the house and slipped my keys off the hook on the wall. I cringed when the door banged shut. My legs raced to my car. "Where are you?"

"I'm heading to the mine."

I shook my head. "Are you crazy? On foot? You can't walk all the way there in the snow."

"I know what's going on. I know who's been doing this. I just need proof."

"Doing what? You aren't making any sense." I opened the door to the Bug and jumped inside, hoping it wouldn't be too loud when I started the engine. It needed to run a bit and warm up.

Rylee sighed. "I'm pretty sure I know who's done this. Have you been listening to the radio?"

My hand paused mid-air, holding the key just millimeters from the ignition. "No. I try to avoid excess noises."

"The body... at the mine," she began whispering again. "It's Kieran's dad. It's all over the news."

"What?" The word echoed inside the small car and against my chest. It'd come out louder than I planned. "That's impossible. He's in Scotland."

"Who told you that? Kieran?"

Obviously. "His dad's been sending him money so he can't be dead." I sighed and stuck the keys into the ignition. "You're my best friend. Please don't be—"

"I'm not jealous! Well, I was, but I'm totally over it." She paused, maybe listening for something or someone. "You need to put your feelings for him aside and think about what I'm saying. It makes sense. Totally."

"Go back home, Rylee." This time I didn't try to hide the irritation in my voice.

"Listen to me! What if Kieran's responsible for all the break-ins and robberies? What if he said the money was from his dad when it wasn't? What if he killed his dad?"

"And broke into Brent's place and hurt his dad?" I sighed dramatically. "He wouldn't hurt his friends. Your brain's on overdrive." I dropped back against the cold seat and shivered. Impossible. Right?

"Something's up and I'm going to prove it."

I leaned forward and started the Bug, shoving it into reverse before I could change my mind. "I'm coming to get you. We'll check things out, together, in the morning." I steered the Bug in the direction of the mine, needing to correct my tires against the frozen road. There was now ice under the freshly fallen snow. "What street are you on?"

Another dramatic-Rylee sigh. "Fine. I'm only saying yes so I can sit in your car. It's freezing." I caught the sound of chattering teeth. "I'm on Phillips."

"I'll be there shortly. I can't talk and drive." As I spoke, black ice on the road had me dropping the phone and grabbing the wheel with both hands.

The phone slipped under my boot but hadn't disconnected. Rylee spoke, "I'll head toward the four-way stop so it's easier to find me. Give me a sec to see how far away I am. I keep gauging distance wrong since I can see everything so crystal clear. It messes up my head."

Her footsteps echoed through the phone as she walked. I heard the sound of a revving engine and crunching tires against the snow through the phone probably before Rylee did. I envisioned some car losing control and smacking into her. "Watch out!" I cried a moment before the awful sound of impact ricocheted out of the phone.

I squeezed the wheel in terror with one hand, and reached down to grab the phone with my other. "Rylee!" I screamed.

Silence. Dead silence. Then spurring of tires and a loud engine disappearing.

Hands shaking on the steering wheel, I stared blankly at the road in front of me. I should turn my windshield wipers on. The defrost had cleared them but the falling snow made things blurry. My thoughts switched to autopilot. I flicked the wipers on and cranked up the heat. Then my brain woke up.

"No! No, no no!" I screamed.

I slowed the car in the middle of the road. No one was around. Reaching around on the floor, I located my cell and dialled 911. Setting it on speaker, I tossed it on the passenger seat and began driving again.

"Nine. One. One. What is your emergency?"

"My friend. I was just on the phone with her. She was walking outside. In the snow. I think she just got hit. By a car."

Still in a daze, I answered the lady's questions, all the while wondering if she actually believed me. None of it made sense.

I pulled onto Phillips and began scanning the sidewalks, also looking for tracks in the snow of a car veering. "Come on, come on, come on, come on," I mumbled. At a stop sign, I speed dialled Dad's house. "Dad!" I shouted when he picked up. "I think Rylee's been hit." I heard him jump up from his office chair.

"Was that the Bug I heard a few minutes ago?"

"Yeah. Get in your car and help me find her. Please, Daddy."

"I'm on my way." Keys jingled. "Where are you?"

"Phillips, going toward the mine."

"Stay where you are, Zoe. I'll come get you and we'll look together."

I pressed my teeth against my lower lip. "I can't find her. I can't—" I lost my voice when I suddenly caught sight of two trails in the snow, cutting across the road and veering onto the sidewalk near a large snow-covered evergreen planted on an old farmhouse yard. I pulled off to the side and jumped out of the Bug.

Sirens rang out into the night air, letting me know help was on its way. I had no idea how far away they were. My boots filled with snow as I ran. I jumped onto the top of an old trailer tie but had to jump off to avoid nearly hitting the large steel pole-things nailed into them. Searching for my best friend, my eyes provided little help in the near darkness. I tried to hear her breathing. She wasn't in the snow where the tire tracks stopped, or under the tree.

"Rylee! Rylee!"

I paused and cocked my head, forcing all other sounds out and focussed on anything unique.

A strange sound I'd never heard before, like a gurgling and slight popping noise seeped into my ear canals. A terrible thought crossed my mind. *Warm blood melting snow.* "No!" I sobbed and swung left, racing around the tree to the other side.

Rylee lay sprawled on the ground face up, her arms stretched out like she was making a snow angel.

Except she wasn't moving.

My legs gave out and I dropped into the snow, kneeling beside her. Wetness seeped through my jeans. Tears coursed down my cheeks and I hiccupped against the pressure in my chest. With a shaking hand, I reached for her neck to try and find a pulse. The sleeve of my coat caught against something sharp. I reached to unsnag it. My hand brushed against cold metal. *Please no!* I scurried back and fell back into the snow when I realized Rylee had been impaled by a piece of metal sticking out of the old railway tie. Horror filled my insides. I didn't want to look, but couldn't stop myself. Glancing closer, I saw the railway tie under her, just below her shoulders. Her back twisted in an angle that the human body wasn't capable of.

I gagged, scrambling over the tie to throw up. Again and again. My body racked with spasms long after my stomach had emptied its contents. "Rylee!" I moved back to my friend, trying to remember everything Dad had taught me about first aid. *Don't move her body. Don't pull the metal out.*

Shaking from cold and fear, it was next to impossible to get my fingers to press against Rylee's neck for a pulse. My gut knew it was in vain. Her blank eyes started up at the sky and her mouth hung slightly open. I covered my face with my hands. Who would do this? It –"

"Zoe!"

I jumped at the sound of a male voice. While focussed on Rylee, I'd somehow managed to tune out every sound.

The evergreen branches shook, sending snow dust flying like sand against my face. Kieran emerged and stopped dead in his tracks. "Holy shit."

Sounds I'd closed off came flooding into my ears, each one racing to get in faster than the other. My sobbing and heavy breathing, Dad talking to someone to get a stretcher, a loud siren now steady as the vehicle was now obviously parked, other people talking and being directed to where Rylee and I were, a policeman trying to get others to stay off the tire tracks, and so much more noise. It was overwhelming.

Kieran raced over to me and pulled me away from Rylee's body. "Let's move away so the medics can help her. You shouldn't be here."

"Sh-Sh-She called. I c-c-couldn't let her go t-to the mine by h-h-herself." My eyes widened as I remembered why Rylee said she needed to go. I went rigid in Kieran's arms, unsure of what to do. *Trust him? Run?*

"She called me, too. I've been running everywhere trying ta find you."

"Zoe?" My dad shouted as he pushed past several paramedics just ahead of him. He smiled with relief when he saw me, then turned to Rylee. "Jeez, no." He shot a look at Kieran. "Get her out of here."

"Yes, sir." Kieran wrapped his arm tightly around me and gently forced me to walk back toward my car. "It's okay," he whispered.

I pulled out of his grasp. "No. It's not! Someone did this to Rylee. Then took off." I squinted at him, thinking about Rylee's last words to me. "Or fled 'cause they were scared. Someone hit her on purpose."

Kieran fidgeted and didn't meet my gaze. "It could've been an accident."

"Then the hit-and-run would have stayed. Called the police. Done the *right* thing." *Was I accusing him?* My chattering teeth seemed to think so. A strange coldness had seeped into my core.

He clasped his hands together and brought them to his forehead. "We need to talk. Not here, with all these people. Let's go sit in the Bug." He pointed at my mouth. "You need to warm up."

He led the way and opened the passenger door for me, then walked around the front of the car and settled into the driver's seat. Once the car started, he cranked the heat and turned the vents on me. "Do you have a blanket in the back or anything?"

I shook my head, absently watching two paramedics run back to their ambulance to grab a gurney and something black. *Kieran couldn't have done this. He's not responsible.*

My dad came into view in front of the headlights. He walked around and tapped on Kieran's window. When Kieran rolled it down, Dad bent forward and looked at me. "You okay, Zoezey?" Without waiting for my reply, he turned to Kieran. "Can you step out a minute?"

Kieran tensed and then relaxed. He patted my knee with one hand and rolled up the window. "Sure."

They must have forgot I could hear them talk, probably too distracted with the horror scene behind the ugly Spruce tree. *Would Dad interrogate Kieran?* What else would he want to talk about out of normal earshot?

"How're things, sir?"

Dad sighed as he rubbed the back of his neck. "Bad. Terrible, actually. Rylee... she... she didn't make it." His voice dropped a few decibels. "They're going to take her body out now. I don't want Zoe here. Her car is parked in full view of the back of the ambulance."

"I'll take her home."

"Thanks. I'm going to be here, then at the hospital, and then talking to Rylee's folks. Can you bring her to her mom's house?"

"Yes, sir."

"Thanks. You're a good kid, Kieran. I appreciate it." Dad shook Kieran's hand and then came around to my side and opened the door. The cool air felt like a slap compared to the quickly warming little car. He squatted down and hugged me.

I buried my face into his shoulder and made no effort to stop the tears or running nose. Kieran opened the driver's door and sat down. He bounced his thumbs idly against the steering wheel. "Daddy, sh-she called m-me. I came out t-to get her... it was too late, wasn't it?" *Ironic.* I could hear everything but right now, even though I knew the truth, I wanted his racing heart, his uneven breathing to be wrong, the words I'd just heard to be a bad dream.

"Shhh..." He stroked my hair. "This isn't your fault. There—"

"Doctor Taylor?" A paramedic called out by the trees. "We, uh, need your help."

Dad leaned away to shout back. "I'll be there in a moment." He squeezed my hand and spoke quietly. "Kieran's going to take you home. Will you be okay?" His voice cracked.

My superman-dad; torn between doing his duty and protecting his daughter. I wasn't hurt – at least physically. "It's fine. I'll be all right. Just really shaken up." I shuddered and pulled my hand from his and lightly pressed my fingers against my throat feeling my heart beat against my skin. It made me think how Rylee's heart would never beat again. I swallowed hard. "I don't think I'll ever get the image out of my head." In a shaking, halting voice I added, "There's no way this was an accident. We need to find out who did this."

Kieran coughed. Tapping of his fingers against the steering wheel began to grate on my ears.

"The police will." Her dad stood. "Let me do my job and let's talk as soon as I get back from the hospital. Kieran's going to drive you to Mom's."

Numb, I nodded and let him lean in to click the seatbelt around me. Kieran revved the engine and slowly pulled the Bug around the ambulance. I stared blankly out the window and watched my dad turn and head back to the paramedics and police standing by the evergreen.

The tree was massive. It had to be at least fifty, sixty years old. I blinked, not sure why I would focus on it. My brain seemed scattered all over the place. I couldn't think straight. "Do you mind if we drive around for a bit?" I needed to concentrate, clear my head.

Kieran flipped the heat on full. "Sure. Where do you want to go?"

I sighed. "I don't care. Maybe somewhere open, where we could walk. I need silence and fresh air."

Kieran shifted in his seat and drove slowly. When he cleared his throat a second time, I looked over, but he said nothing. He darted several glances in my direction but quickly turned back to focus on the snowy road. I stared at his profile. Rylee said he was responsible for everything. I didn't believe it, I couldn't believe it. *And yet...* I straightened and my body forgot how to breathe. No, it wasn't right. He didn't have it in him.

"This okay?" Kieran rolled the car to a stop and let the engine idle.

Huh? I glanced out the window and realized he'd driven down the road which led to the mine. *Of all the quiet places.* "It's good. Perfect, actually." He understood my need for silence, out here there was only nature, no city noise. I opened my door and stepped into barely enough snow to cover the ground. In the open field, the wind must have blown the snow so little accumulated.

I walked around to the driver's side of the car and then continued on, following the path of less snow. Kieran walked quietly beside me, his hand stuffed deep into his pockets. I turned to check if the headlights for the Bug were still on. Just before they automatically shut off, I caught a glimmer of something steel. I paused, letting my eyes adjust and squinted into the darkness. My stomach dropped. "Is that your bike? What's it doing here?"

It took him too long to reply.

"You bastard!" I turned in disbelief. "*You* did this?"

Chapter 16

The silence grew deafening. I covered my ears in the hopes of drowning everything out. *Impossible.* The truth screamed louder than any super-sonar sound I'd heard since that stormy night in the mine. It felt like déjà vu to be standing just outside of it now.

Whatever shock I'd felt moments ago flew out the window. Sadness settled all over me. I wished I could just squeeze my eyes tight and pretend it was all a bad dream. I whispered, finally peering at him through my eyelashes, "Rylee knew... she tried to tell me... how could you?"

"Does it matter?" Kieran stood stock-still, not even blinking. The mine behind appeared to be laughing. *At me? At him? Or both of us?*

One of my hands found its way to the side of my face, my fingertips pushing against my temple. His words bounced inside my head. *Did it matter?* He couldn't take anything back, so why should it? "If-If you brought yourself in... you could..." I didn't know what I was trying to say, or even how to say it. "Y-You could get h-help." *Deep down you're not bad.* I dropped my arm and intertwined my fingers, like they were trying to pray.

Kieran brought his hand to my face. His thumb rubbed lightly against my cheek. Staring me directly in the eyes, his shoulders rose and fell. His voice came out soft, almost regretful. "Not everyone can be helped. Some of us are just too damaged."

My heart melted, just a tiny bit. "No you're not."

He laughed. It came out sarcastic... bitter. "You don't know me."

"I thought I did." Boy had I been wrong. *Could I be in the way of his agenda now?* I stepped back, glancing toward the Beetle. There was no way I could run over, climb in, get it started, and pull away before he would catch up. The horrid mine was my only other option.

"You thought you knew me?" He shook his head, sweeping his free arm wide. "Everyone's senses got mashed that night and, not for one moment, did you even consider me? I was brushed aside like a useless git."

"No..." I wracked my brain but he was right, in a sense. "We just figured, five senses – five of us." I pointed at him. "You never admitted it that night at PHP, when all of us did. You said it was 'cause we all grew up here. Why didn't you tell us?"

"I never knew!" He crushed his fingers through his hair. "I had the bad headache, but 'ow was I supposed to know I'd inherited a freaky-strong sixth sense? I didn't believe it meself."

"But..." My brain couldn't wrap itself fully around this. "You did bloodwork. My dad never said anything."

"He couldn't have. I switched it. The front desk lady never saw me." He tapped his head. "It was so easy knowing how with this."

"When did you figure it out?" I thought back to the first day I came to his house. A thought struck me. I closed my eyes a moment and then met his gaze. I couldn't believe how I'd missed it. "I think I know. The day I met your dad, and almost knocked over your mom's Scottish thistle. You reacted before I barely thought about touching it." More memories crowded my mind. His perfectly timed smiles, the way he seemed to know exactly what I was thinking, or what to say. The night at the water tower. He knew I'd make it down. Then how he knew the hyperbaric chamber would work. Bile filled my throat, and I swallowed in disgust. He'd known and never told me, even as we grew closer. "All of this... me and you... was just a game to you? Try and see how fast you can get the blond to fall for you? I—"

"You were never a game." He stepped toward me, which only made me cringe. He swore under his breath. *"Shite!"*

It shouted loud and clear in my ears. His heart hammered at car-wrecking speed. I waited while he inhaled long, deep breaths. That incredible body, I'd dreamt so many nights about, composed itself – inside and out.

His voice came out quiet and steady. Deadly. "One mistake." He lifted his pointer finger to the sky. "Me dad gets his sorry-ass drunk, an' I git in his way."

I pressed my lips tight together. My stomach dropped with the fear of hearing his next words.

"Did you know 'e was in the British Army? Undercover ops. All the terrorist shite after nine-eleven. When me mum died, he was gone. Not working, just gone. Didn't come back till four months after we buried her. I," he jabbed a finger at his chest, "had to bury her alone. At eleven years old. The bank took the house. Everything! Then I had to stay with neighbours. The bloody neighbours!" He began pacing, his body becoming tense again. "You know what he did to me *that* night?"

I stared as he walked, too shocked to speak. *You lost your mother to cancer and your dad didn't come back?*

"No, he didn't," he said, sensing my thoughts, "and when 'e finally did, 'e couldn't even look at me. Spent every minute with his hand wrapped around a damn bottle. Unless he was trying to wrap it around my neck. Couldn't face up and be a man. He just ran away and ended up 'ere." Kieran stopped moving and turned his head sharply to gaze at me. "Tha' first night after training, an' I went to git my bike, he came after me. Twisted me arm and held a gun to my head. Drunk bastard shoved me in the trunk of his car and drove me out to the mine. To here! He was gonna execute me. He said I killed his wife."

"No," I whispered, my brows high against my forehead. I pictured him beaten and scared, dragged out of the trunk and forced to his knees. His father just as menacing as the mine. My stomach rolled with the fear he must have felt.

"I'd always managed to handle him but..." He shuddered. "That nigh', he 'ad this look in his eyes. I didn't know what ta do."

"Then it was self-defence."

Kieran's eyebrows shot up. "You beautiful, stupid girl." He came over and gently rested a hand on my shoulder. "No one would believe that. You heard wha' they said 'bout the body. It was rage. I hated 'im for letting me mum suffer and die alone. Then I hated 'im more for coming back a shell of the man—the hero—I believed 'e was."

My eyes filled, thinking of the Kieran as a little boy, so lost and afraid.

"Iye. Leave the past alone. I can't bring them back." He snorted. "No one can trace me back to 'is death." He tucked a stray strand of hair behind my ear, tracing its outer rim with his finger. "No one knows, 'cept you." A smile which first seemed a warning turned tender. "I'd never 'urt you. *Ever.*"

Part of me believed him. However, the sane part told me to get out of there as fast as I could.

He leaned forward, his lips brushing lightly against mine before he leaned close to my ear. "You cannit run. I'll always find you." His breath, hot against my neck, scorched down my spine. "We're meant to be together."

I stiffened. He didn't own me. "No we're not. You killed Rylee. You belong in jail." I shoved him away and then stuffed my hands into my coat pocket, reaching for my Blackberry.

"I didn—Don't dial nine-nine-nine. You'll regret it." He held out his hand, his fingers flipping, telling me to give him the phone.

"I wasn't going to." That didn't officially constitute as a lie. I'd have dialled nine-one-one, not the British emergency number. I paused when a distinct sound in the distance caught my attention. A high revving sound. *A vehicle hurdling down the road toward us.*

Someone else had figured it out.

Kieran grabbed and pulled me tight, kissing me again on the lips. Rougher this time, like someone scared. Terrified he might not see me again. "I'll find you. Don't worry, I will." He squeezed my hand one last time, then ran over to his bike and jumped on. His helmet disappeared from the handle bar and was on his head before I had a chance blink. "Tell Brent," He grinned, as if he knew some private joke. "Tell 'im ta take care of you till I come back."

I cowered and flinched when his motorbike roared to life. Dirt and grass sputtered from his back wheel as he took off and disappeared into the night. The scream of his engine disappeared in the opposite direction of the other car coming toward the mine.

Then I did what any normal teenage girl would do. I started crying. I fell to ground on my knees and covered my face in my hands, letting the sobs rack through my body. Relief. Rage. Love. Shattered heart. Emotions coursed through my body and all I could do was weep. Wet snow seeped through my jeans but I ignored the cold.

My sonar hearing audibly told me the car, racing toward the mine, had skidded to a stop close by my Beetle. The driver's door opened and running shoes padded against the dry grass. I knew the rhythm of those feet.

Warm, comforting arms circled around me from behind. I heard Brent's heart and allowed myself to collapse against him.

"Shh..." He held me tight. "You're okay. Right? You're not hurt – physically, I mean?"

I nodded, turning around to bury my face in his shoulder. He smelled like sweat, Gillette deodorant, and some kind of guitar wax or polish he always used. I loved him for it – for not changing or hiding things from me.

He held me and never said a word. Just let me blubber away until I leaned back and wiped my nose with the sleeve of my coat.

"Sorry." I stood. "No Kleenex."

Smiling, he stuffed his hands into his pockets. I could hear his fingers dance against the material of his coat. "He's gone?" He glanced behind me.

"Yeah. We won't be able to catch him." I sniffed, trying to prevent my wet nose from running again. "No one will."

"What?" His eyebrows rose.

"He's got an ability as well." I released a shaky sigh.

Brent didn't look surprised, like he'd already figured it out.

"It's a sixth sense."

He frowned. "What do we do?"

"Run. Hide. I don't know." Realistically, I was the only one who needed to hide. He only wanted me.

Brent's jaw tightened. "Where do you want to go? Wherever it is, I'll come with you." His eyes suddenly seemed to look a lot older than seventeen years. "I can protect you."

Always the soldier of protection. "Somewhere Kieran would never think to look." An owl hooted and the tree branches clacked against each other as the wind picked up. Snow fell from the trees in muffled drops.

The noises of the night came back alive. Could all of me?

Chapter 17

The local paper ran Rylee's death like it was the most exciting thing in Elliot Lake. They used horrible photos of the ambulance, her body on a gurney, the tree and then pictures of the tree after the farmer had cut it down and left a tall stump. The reporter wrote how the farmer couldn't look at the spruce and see beauty in it anymore, all he could see what the mangled body of a young girl.

I tried to avoid the papers but I'd see a copy on the table or Dad's desk and be unable to turn away. The day the stump photo covered the front page I must have squealed or cried out of something. Dad came running into the room. "Are you okay?"

The laugh that came out of me sounded hysterical or something you'd expect to hear from a crazy person. It was the morning of the funeral and I'd stepped into Dad's office to grab a pen. I'd bought a card for Rylee's parents and wanted to add a note. "The picture. Have you seen it?"

He nodded, his mouth set in a grim line.

I waved my hand. "No, did you see *our* picture? The paper's got some excess red ink on it. The tree looks like it's bleeding. Like blood is coming out of the cuts. Like tears of blood from being cut down. It's awful." Angry at not noticing the tears coursing down my cheeks sooner, I swiped them off my face.

Dad stared at me, then at the paper clenched in my hands and then back to my face. "It's just a bad ink run. It's not..." His words trailed off, even he didn't know what to say.

"Forget it." I stuffed the paper under my armpit and stepped around him to get out the door. "Mom's outta the shower and I need to finish my hair." Mom and I had slept over at Dad's since the accident. I knew they were sleeping in his room together but didn't say anything.

We all were keeping secrets these days.

Inside the bathroom and behind the locked door I glared at the image in the mirror and then dissolved into tears. How in the world do you bury one of your best friends? Rylee would never graduate, go to university, be a pageant queen – she'd have made a darn good one, she'd never get married or have kids. Her parents wouldn't know if their grandbabies looked like her or anything.

Mom's soft footsteps stopped by the bathroom. She didn't say anything, just stood behind it with sad, long breaths. I heard her sigh and Dad whisper from down the hall, "Give her a moment. She'll be okay."

I straightened and grabbed tissue to blow my noise. You'd think I'd have run out of tears after the past few days, but the well never seemed to run dry. I pulled my hair of out its bun and wore it down, the way Rylee liked it. The black dress I wore was the one Rylee had bought me for my birthday. A bit cold to wear something sleeveless but my mom let me borrow a fancy expensive scarf she had and I wore it over my shoulders like a shawl. It matched perfectly. Rylee would have loved it.

The lump in my throat needed to go. I swallowed hard and went to get my boots.

We drove to the funeral in silence. Entering the church through a side door, I heard Brent, Seth, and Heidi before I saw them. "Mom, I'm going to find my friends." I trudged toward their quiet voices before either of my parents could reply.

Brent found me just before I turned the corner at the end of the hall. He hugged me tight. "You okay?" he whispered.

"I'm managing. What about you?"

He sighed. "It sucks." His lips brushed against the top of my head and he held me tighter.

I let my weight lean into him. I could hear people whispering in the sanctuary and other students gossiping. No one knew about our abilities. At least if they did, no one was talking about it. I tuned the whispers out and as I did, I thought about Kieran and how he had figured out how to get me to do it in the hyperbaric chamber. Fresh tears came to my eyes. Thank goodness for waterproof mascara. I pressed my face against Brent's chest and tried to muffle the cry.

He continued to hold me and stroked my hair.

Seth and Heidi came and stood by us. I gave Brent another tight squeeze and straightened so I could hug Heidi. We started crying all over again.

My father appeared in the hallway with a large box in his hand. "Zoezey?" He cleared his throat. "This just arrived for you by UPS." He opened a door to a nearby room and set it on a table.

I followed and tried to think of who would send something here, today. Dad offered his Swiss Army knife and I cut open the box. There was another one inside with a note taped on top of it.

I gasped. The note wasn't signed but I knew who wrote it.

Zoe,

Please take care of this. I want the two most precious things in my life together.

With shaking hands, I opened the second box and moved aside the packing peanuts. Wrapped in bubble wrap lay a Waterford crystal Scottish thistle.

"Who's the crystal from?" Seth asked, leaning over my shoulder. Heidi stood on my other side.

I closed the box, hoping they wouldn't figure out the shape inside the bubble wrap was a Scottish thistle. "I'm not sure. Probably an aunt or something."

My father's eyebrow rose but he didn't say anything. Thank goodness. He stepped forward. "Why don't I put this in the trunk of my car for now?" He gathered the box and carried it out of the room.

Brent checked his watch. "The memorial is going to be starting soon. They've reserved a row for us by Ry-Rylee's parents." He swallowed hard.

Seth leaned over to Brent and clasped him on the shoulder. "We are going to find Kieran and make him pay."

Heidi pulled away from beside me. Her face sad but more determined than I had ever seen it. "We'll find him. Stupid sixth sense can't see all five..." she choked on the last word, "I mean four of us, coming after him."

I stared at my three friends, my heart torn in every direction.

Unlike the others, I didn't care about revenge. I had no stake in the outcome of Kieran's life or his future.

It's hard, I thought, blinking back the tears. *I wanted to believe people could change, even people who are damaged.* I inhaled long and deep, then released it slowly.

But I don't know if they can. I just don't know.

THE END

... For now

NONSENSE, the third installment of the Senseless Series, coming Summer 2014

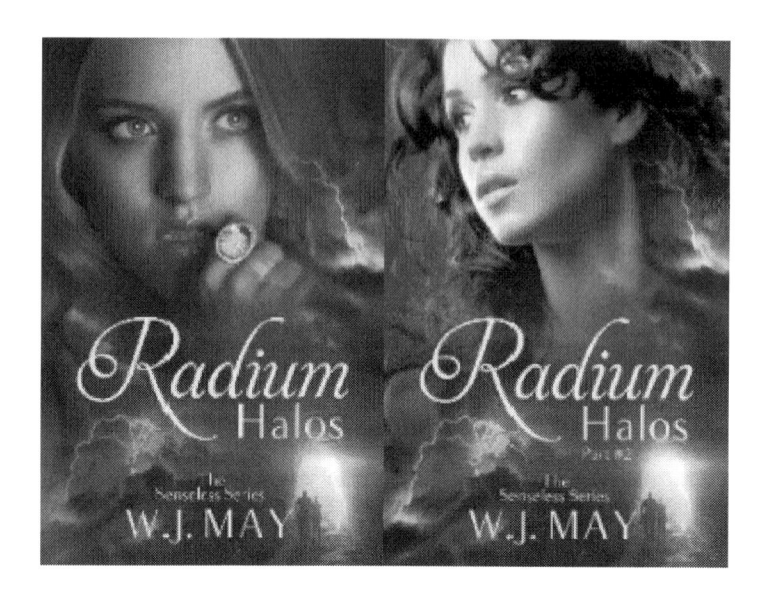

I hope you enjoyed Radium Halos. I love to hear from readers so please feel free to contact me or post a line or two review so others can find the series!

Looking forward to see you for part 2, NONSENSE,
W.J. May

MORE BOOKS BY W.J. MAY:

THE CHRONICLES OF KERRIGAN

Book Trailer:

http://www.youtube.com/watch?v=gILAwXxx8MU

BOOK BLURB:

How hard do you have to shake the family tree to find the truth about the past?

Fifteen year-old Rae Kerrigan never really knew her family's history. Her mother and father died when she was young and it is only when she accepts a scholarship to the prestigious Guilder Boarding School in England that a mysterious family secret is revealed.

Will the sins of the father be the sins of the daughter?

As Rae struggles with new friends, a new school and a star-struck forbidden love, she must also face the ultimate challenge: receive a tattoo on her sixteenth birthday with specific powers that may bind her to an unspeakable darkness. It's up to Rae to undo the dark evil in her family's past and have a ray of hope for her future.

** FREE CHAPTER EXCERPT **

The Chronicles of Kerrigan

Rae of Hope
by
W.J. May
Copyright 2012 by W.J. May

http://www.wanitamay.yolasite.com
Facebook Page:
https://www.facebook.com/pages/Author-WJ-May-FAN-PAGE
Cover design by: Patrick Griffith

The Chronicles of Kerrigan
Book I – Rae of Hope Book Trailer:
http://www.youtube.com/watch?v=gILAwXxx8MU
Book II – Dark Nebula Book Trailer:
http://www.youtube.com/watch?v=Ca24STi_bFM
Book III – House of Cards, coming March 2014
Book IV – Royal Tea, coming June 2014

RAE OF HOPE

Chapter 1

Guilder Boarding School

"You can't undo the past. The sins of the father are the sins of the son, or in this case, daughter."

Uncle Argyle's ominous words had echoed in Rae's head long after he dropped her off at the airport. "A proverb of truth" he had called it. Who spoke like that nowadays? *Some good-bye.* Tightening her ponytail and futilely trying to tuck her forever-escaping dark curls behind her ears, she looked at her watch, then out the bus window at the tree lined countryside. It seemed strange to see the sun. All she remembered was rain when she had lived in Britain nine years ago.

Trying to get comfortable, Rae tucked her foot up on the seat, and rested her head against her knee as she looked out at the scenery flashing by. A sign outside the window showed the miles before the bus reached Guilder. It'd be another twenty-five minutes. She popped her ear buds in, blew the bangs away from her forehead and stared out the window across the rolling farm fields, trying to let the music from her iPod distract her.

It didn't work. Just when she felt the tension begin to ease from her shoulders and she started to get into the song, something caught her eye. Black smoke billowed just near the top of a lush green hill. Rae stared, her heart fluttering as an old memory began to take hold. She knew what that smoke meant. She'd seen it before, long ago.

Someone's house was burning.

Crap, crap crap, no I don't want to go there. Her heart started racing and her stomach turned over, making her feel nauseous.

Dropping her knee, she gripped the seat in front of her, burying her face in her hands taking deep breaths, like the therapists taught her to do. She'd gone through years of therapy to treat what had been called "panic attacks". It didn't matter what other people called it. To her, it was simply hell; like being sucked back in time against her will, to a place she never wanted to revisit. So she breathed the way she'd been taught, slow breathe in, all the way, then slow breath out, all the time chanting *it's not real, it's not real* in her head.

It helped calm her racing heart and made her feel more in control, but it didn't erase the memory. Nothing on Earth could do that. Being back in England for the first time and seeing the strange smoke, Rae felt six years old all over again.

She'd been in the living room coloring with new markers before bed when her mother told her to take them to the tree house her dad had built for her and play there until she called her in. That call never came. The blaze bounced horrific shadows around the inside of the tree house. The stinky black smoke slithered in and scared her little six year old self in ways the monsters under her bed never had.

Rae shuddered and lurched upright, forcefully bringing herself back to the present. *Could this school be any further into the sticks?*

Glancing around the now vacant bus, she wondered if the driver had purposely left her until last. She'd watched the last few people get off at a school about fifteen minutes ago, Roe-something or other. They all looked the same, all pretty girls with blonde hair, not one of them thin, pale, and tall like her. They hadn't been friendly. *Big surprise there...* She was used to it. She tended to fly under the radar at best. So she handled them the way she always handled the ones who instantly didn't like her for no reason she could come up with. Rae avoided making eye contact and tried to appear immersed in the Guilder Boarding School brochure. It wasn't that she didn't want to make friends. She'd just never really had any. Most kids her age either didn't like her or didn't notice her.

It bugged her that Uncle Argyle had pushed so hard for her to go when Guilder sent the letter. He'd been the one to move them all from Scotland to New York when she'd come to live with them, taking her away from the horrible tragedy of her parents' death, and now, he suddenly leapt at the chance for her to go back? It didn't make any sense. It sort of sucked to leave her current high school. She lacked close friends, but she also lacked enemies, which was a plus in her book. The girls there seemed just as stuck up as the ones who'd gotten off the bus earlier, but they'd simply ignored her. Rae always told herself it didn't matter anyway. Cliques were *so passé* in her opinion.

Another weird thing that she couldn't seem to find an answer to was why Guilder would choose her? How did they even know she existed? Her uncle boasted how big a deal it was for her to be selected, but he'd never once explained how they'd even come to know about her in the first place. She had the grades, the brain part always came easy for her, but she didn't have any extra-curricular activities at all, nothing to make her stand out. So, how had this amazing school she'd never heard of before decide to take her on? It didn't make any sense. She tried a few times before she left to corner her uncle and get him to explain part or all of it, but he'd always seemed to be busy.

While this wasn't exactly abnormal behavior for him, it still left her with a sense of foreboding, something that had clung to her ever since she got the letter. She couldn't figure out why, but she had a strong sense that something big was coming. Whether it was good or bad, she didn't know.

A movement out of the corner of her eye caught her attention, pulling her mind out of the endless circle of questions in her head. She turned to look out the window, and was stunned to see the largest bird she'd ever seen in her life. *Maybe an eagle?* The thing flew parallel with the bus, right beside her. Pressing her face against the cool glass, her gaze focused intently on the curious sight. She jerked back when its large wings flapped, brushed the window, and then veered away. She watched its graceful flight as it soared and then swooped to settle onto the limb of a large tree just ahead. As the bus passed by, the bird seemed to lock eyes with Rae and she was mesmerized. Rae had always wondered what it would feel like to be a bird, to fly so free, go anywhere the wind took her. She continued to watch the bird until she couldn't see it anymore, then slumped back into her seat as the bus sped onward down the long road.

Guilder Boarding School. She gnawed at the cuticle on her thumbnail a little too hard and ripped the skin, drawing a wince from her. She couldn't help it, she always did this when she was nervous. She'd be the only American girl. *Well, not really American.* She held a British passport but had moved to New York after her parents died in the fire, leaving her orphaned. So...not really American, not really British; a little of both, but belonging to neither.

The bus cruised by an aged stone sign. *Guilder Boarding School, Founded 1520. One of Britain's Finest Educational Institutions.* Rae read the sign and wondered how a school could be that old and not be featured in stories or online. She found nothing when she tried researching it. They drove under an old, leaded window arch that connected two round, red-brick towers. The stream of people coming and going from the doors at the bottom made her think it must be some kind of office. She craned her neck to get a better view. The buildings were old but were well kept and held an almost magical aura of their original Tudor era. She half expected to see men in tights and codpieces strutting down the road, leading their horses, with corseted ladies perched delicately atop them. The mental picture amused her and she absent-mindedly smiled. Her eyes were drawn to the ornate, brick chimneys along the buildings' roofs. She glimpsed the other buildings beyond. *This place looks huge...hope I don't get lost.*

The driver pulled to a halt in front of a building with an embossed plaque that said "Aumbry House". The ancient building had ivy growing all over it. It looked like it was probably older than Henry VIII, leaving Rae with horrifying visions of chamber pots dancing in her head. *It better have indoor plumbing...*

The bus door slid open with a hiss. Rae gathered her two small suitcases and her book bag, clambered down the aisle and finally, blessedly, off the bus.

"Welcome to Guilder, Ms. Kerrigan." Rae awkwardly spun around to face the voice, finding that a tall, thin woman stood on the concrete steps of the building, her eyes darting left and right, pausing on Rae for barely more than a few seconds.

Rae stared, wondering where the lady had come from. *She wasn't there a moment ago.* Rae looked at the woman's long, wool skirt. *This might be England, but today is sweltering. How is she not melting in this heat?*

"I am Madame Elpis, your house mistress." The lady darted down the large concrete steps, pausing on the last step and, in one fluid motion, tucked her clip board under an armpit and extended her hand.

The woman's features reminded Rae of a bird – her jet-black hair, dark eyes, and especially the jutting nose. Rae nodded and dropped a suitcase so she could return the handshake, her fingers crushed by the woman's claw-like grip. *Ow, ow, ow! So you're freakishly strong, got it.*

"Come along. No time for dilly-dallying." She turned and marched up the steps, not checking to see if Rae followed or needed any help with her bags.

Huffing out a breath, Rae grabbed her things and clambered to follow, hearing the bus driver chuckle as he closed the door behind her. *I'm spending the next two years here? What joy; What freakin' bliss.*

Hammering and drilling noises from above greeted Rae as she came through the entrance. The clamor echoed throughout the building.

"Fifteen and sixteen-year-olds are on the second floor," Madame Elpis shouted above the noise. "Your room is the last door on the left." She checked the chart she'd been holding under her arm. "Molly Skye is your roommate. I assume you can find the way." The last part was more statement than question.

"Thank you," Rae replied uncertainly, not knowing what else to say.

Madame Elpis pointed to a door on her left. "The study hall's through there. The glass doors lead to the game room. The door to your right is to my living quarters. You are not permitted there." She led Rae to the winding staircase made of black and white marble. "Juniors are on the second floor, seniors on the third and fourth." She glanced at an old pocket watch hanging on a chain around her neck and, if possible, straightened even more. "Dinner is at five o'clock, sharp." She turned, her skirt swirling as she darted into her room, and with a kick of her boot, slammed the door.

Rae exhaled the breath she hadn't realize she'd been holding. The banging of hammers and screeching whine of electric saws reverberated through the hallway. She was so nervous, the hammering could have been coming from her heart and she wouldn't have been able to tell the difference.

Rae took her time up the marble stairs and, once on the landing, headed left to the end of the hall. Biting the inside of her cheek, she gave a light knock at the slightly open door and peered in. *Empty.* Rae cautiously pushed the door open and surveyed her new room.

Thick, lush brown carpet covered the floor. Two beds, with matching duvets and tan suede pillows, rested against the opposing walls. One of which already sat full of half-empty suitcases. Modern closets with ample space matched perfectly with the antique desks built into the wall by each oriel window. Rae inhaled deeply, taking in a mingled sense of fresh paint and the unique scent of antiques.

Finally! It'd been one helluva long day of traveling. Much of the tension ebbed from her shoulders and she cracked a smile for the first time in hours.

Rae dropped her suitcases on the uncluttered side of the room. Her roommate, Molly, must have stepped out halfway through unpacking. Her closet doors were spread open, with hangers already full of clothes and more shoes than Rae had owned in her entire life. She'd never been big on dressing up, but she still knew designer labels when she saw them and she saw an awful lot of them in that closet. Hopefully, her roommate didn't end up being superficial. Rae stood there wondering how she'd deal with it if she had to room with Guilder's Next Super Model. Visions of her roommate stomping up and down the room in heels practicing her "walk" distracted her. She didn't hear the footsteps walking down the hall to the door.

"What are you doing in me room?" Rae jumped and dropped her purse. A fashionably dressed girl stood in the doorway. She had dark, mahogany red hair, the kind women paid insane amounts of money to try to copy. *Oh great…well, here we go.*

"Molly?" Rae swallowed. "I'm your new roommate."

Molly stared Rae up and down. "You're Rae Kerrigan? I pictured someone totally different. You're not scary at all!" She laughed as if at some private joke. *Scary? Me? What is she talking about?*

"Name's Molly Skye. I'm from Cardiff, in Wales." She shoved one of her suitcases onto the floor and dropped into the small, open space on the bed.

Rae watched, confused. Why would anyone think of her as scary? Because she lived in New York? She had a terrible premonition of being the odd one out, and school hadn't even started yet.

"You're not sixteen, eh? No ta'too?" Molly pointedly dropped her gaze down to Rae's waist, as if she expected Rae to show her something.

Tattoo? Rae squinted, trying to listen closer to Molly's accent. The way she spoke, some of the words were hard to make out. *Why would she ask if I have a tattoo?*

"My birthday's in three days. It's going to be so awesome!" Molly leaned back on her elbows. "When's yers?"

"My birthday? Uh...not 'til November." *Straight into the personal info. Okay, I think I know what my roommate is going to be like.*

"November? You do have a long wait." Molly grimaced and shook her head. "Poor you. You'll be the last one inked for sure." She jumped off the bed. Rae noted the strange comment, but Molly's motor-mouth went speeding on, so she filed it away for examination at a later time.

"What'd you think of our room? Pretty cool, eh? Aside from the construction on the floors above us." She shot the ceiling an annoyed look. "I just talked to one of the workers. He said they finish at four. They start again at like eight in the morning! Can you believe that? Who gets up at that time, anyway?"

Wow. Molly can talk without pausing for breath. Rae nodded and tried to keep up. She watched Molly roll from the balls of her feet to her heels, back and forth continually. It was a typically nervous gesture that Rae attributed to meeting new people. *Everybody has their issues, but it's still surprising, considering how fast she's talking.*

"Can you believe we got invited to Guilder? We're two of sixteen females within a landmass of rich, supposedly unattainable, handsome boys." When Rae didn't respond, Molly squinted at her.

"You do know why you're here, right?"

Rae shrugged. Jet lag seemed to be eating her brain cells. "To be honest, I don't really know what you mean. I haven't been in England since I was six and I know nothing about Guilder." *Despite numerous Google searches at home and having my nose buried in the brochure for an hour on the ride here.*

"You're not slow or something, are you?" Rae shook her head slowly wondering if her talkative new roomie had just insulted her. Molly stared, scratching her head. "You really don't know, do you?" She looked up and to the left, obviously recalling something important. She straightened, as if quoting some bit of brochure from memory. "Guilder's a highly sought after educational institution, but it is primarily a school for the gifted. People who get to go to Guilder know why. The rest of the world has no idea!"

Rae curled her fingers tight, her nails digging into her palms. She felt stupid and also irritated at herself for feeling stupid. It wasn't something she wanted to deal with, especially after such a long day of travel. "What makes us...gifted?"

Molly's eyes grew huge. She paced the room. "Oh, my... Me da's never going to believe this. You seriously don't know ANYTHING?!"

Rae felt her blood pressure rising. She knew she was tired, confused, and nervous. None of that it was helping her temper, but she was determined not to lose it on what amounted to a total stranger. She pressed her lips tight to stop any snappish comment that might escape. *Can't the ditz just answer a simple question with a straight answer?*

Molly swung around in front of Rae, dramatically squared her shoulders, and put on a serious face. "When we turn sixteen, we receive our ink blot."

"What?"

"A ta'too." She leaned forward and whispered, "It gives us special powers."

Pause...say what? "P-Powers?" Rae tried not to laugh. Had her uncle sent her to an institution for the insane? "You're kidding, right?" Uncle Argyle had told her the experience would change her life, but hadn't said how. Rae figured he meant she'd do some growing up – like a maturity thing. And, of course, there was that silly proverb. But perhaps he'd mistakenly sent her off to a giant rubber room.

Molly waved a hand. "I'm serious. The gift is passed down from generation to generation." She blew out an exaggerated breath. "Any guy around here who's sixteen has a ta'too on the inside of his forearm." She dragged Rae toward the window and pointed to the building across from them. "That's the boys' dorm. Let's go outside and walk around. I'll get one of them to show you what I mean."

Her eyes dropped down to Rae's clothes, her lips pursed tight together. "Do you fancy a quick change before we go?"

Rae laughed, despite her roommate's serious expression. Molly definitely was crazy, but she had a point. She'd dressed comfortably for travel, and even though she wasn't big on fashion, even she drew the line at meeting her new classmates looking like a worked-over hag. She could use some freshening-up. "Yeah, give me a moment."

"I'm off downstairs to try and find some cute boys. Meet me outside when you're ready." Molly left, still chattering nonstop with no one in the hall to listen.

Rae opened the closest suitcase and grabbed the first pair of jeans and top within reach. She hesitated and dug a little deeper into her suitcase. The jeans were fine, they were new, but a white t-shirt seemed too plain. She found a pink Converse tank top with ONE STAR written in sparkles. She pulled out her hair tie, wishing her unruly black curls were straight like Molly's perfect hair. She never bothered with makeup because she had crazy-long eyelashes that mascara seemed to only want to clomp up against, and almost everything else just made her look kinda like a sloppy hooker. *Keep it simple,* that's what her aunt had always told her. She settled for lip gloss, and deodorant, and then grabbed a pair of sandals before tossing her purse under her pillow. *Now, time to find out what Molly's been babbling on about, or at least, maybe meet some cute guys.* She might be invisible most of the time, but eye candy was eye-candy, no matter which side of the Atlantic it was seen on.

Once outside, she shaded her eyes against the bright sunlight with her hand and searched for her new roommate.

Molly stood further down the sidewalk, talking to a very hot guy with chestnut brown hair, dark eyes and a dimple on his right cheek. It disappeared when he stopped smiling and began talking again, making Rae a little sad. She wanted to see that dimple again. Rae bounded down the steps, and then slowed down, trying not to appear too excited. She flinched and covered her head when a loud crashing noise sounded from above, and a large piece of debris flew down from the fourth floor and landed in the blue bin beside her. Face burning, she pretended it hadn't bothered her and continued walking. Molly and the boy turned to stare in her direction.

Rae heard someone holler from above, but couldn't make out what the guy said. Embarrassed by her reaction a moment before, she ignored the shout and kept walking. Molly's eyes grew big, her hands flew to her cheeks and her mouth dropped open. She screamed. Rae stared as Molly frantically pointed above her head. Rae tipped her head up. She froze in horror when she saw a huge, severed piece of wood paneling balanced like a seesaw on the window ledge several floors above.

The wood scraped against the windowsill, and teetered as if undecided which way it should fall. *Oh crap!* A gust of hot, dry wind blew by, knocking the severed beam into final decent. It spun as it fell and all sound was just gone.

Fight or flight. Rae dropped her gaze, her eyes darted about. The guy beside Molly moved toward her frozen frame. Everything moved in slow motion except for the guy running like a freight train. He was greased lightning, moving faster than anything Rae had ever seen. It didn't seem possible for a person to move so fast. *And why am I focused on him when I'm about to be squashed like a bug?*

END OF EXCERPT

You can purchase Rae of Hope for FREE

Shadow of Doubt

Book Trailer: http://www.youtube.com/watch?v=LZK09Fe7kgA

Book Blurb:
What happens when you fall for the one you are forbidden to love?
    Erebus is a bit of a lost soul. He's a guy so he should be out to have fun but unlike the rest of his kind, he is solemn and withdrawn. That is, until he meets Aurora, a law student at Cornell University. His entire world is shaken. Feelings he's never had and urges he's never understood take over. These strange longings drive

him to question everything about himself.

When a jealous ex stalks back into his life, he must decide if he is willing to risk everything to be with Aurora. His desire for her could destroy her, or worse, erase his own existence forever.

Free Books:

COMING SOON:

Book Blurb:

What if courage was your only option?

When Kallie lands a college interview with the city's new hot-shot police officer, she has no idea everything in her life is about to change. The detective is young, handsome and seems to have an unnatural ability to stop the increasing local crime rate. Detective Liam's particular interest in Kallie sends her heart and head stumbling over each other.

When a raging blood feud between vampires spills into her home, Kallie gets caught in the middle. Torn between love and family loyalty she must find the courage to fight what she fears the most and possibly risk everything, even if it means dying for those she loves.

Seventh Mark
W.J. May

W. J. May
SEVENTH
MARK
The Hidden Secrets Saga

Hidden Secrets Saga:

Download Seventh Mark part 1 For FREE

Book Trailer:
http://www.youtube.com/watch?v=Y-_vVYC1gvo

Book Blurb:

Like most teenagers, Rouge is trying to figure out who she is and what she wants to be. With little knowledge about her past, she has questions but has never tried to find the answers. Everything changes when she befriends a strangely intoxicating family. Siblings Grace and Michael, appear to have secrets which seem connected to Rouge. Her hunch is confirmed when a horrible incident occurs at an outdoor party. Rouge may be the only one who can find the answer.

An ancient journal, a Sioghra necklace and a special mark force life-altering decisions for a girl who grew up unprepared to fight for her life or others.

All secrets have a cost and Rouge's determination to find the truth can only lead to trouble...or something even more sinister.

Did you love *Radium Halos - Part 2*? Then you should read *Four and a Half Shades of Fantasy* by W.J. May!

Four (and a half) Fantasy/Romance first Books from five different series! From best-selling author, W.J. May comes an anthology of five great fantasy, paranormal and romance stories. Books included: Rae of Hope from The Chronicles of Kerrigan Seventh Mark - Part 1 from the Hidden Secrets Saga Shadow of Doubt - Part 1 Radium Halos from the Senseless Series and an excerpt from Courage Runs Red from the Red Blood Series

Also by W.J. May

Hidden Secrets Saga
Seventh Mark - Part 1
Seventh Mark - Part 2

The Chronicles of Kerrigan
Rae of Hope
Dark Nebula

The Senseless Series
Radium Halos
Radium Halos - Part 2

Standalone
Five Shades of Fantasy
Glow - A Young Adult Fantasy Sampler
Shadow of Doubt - Part 1
Shadow of Doubt - Part 2
Four and a Half Shades of Fantasy

Made in the USA
Charleston, SC
17 March 2014